DANNY ORLIS
AND
ROBIN'S BIG BATTLE

DANNY ORLIS

AND

ROBIN'S BIG BATTLE

BERNARD PALMER

Please note that several books in the Danny Orlis series are published by Sword of the Lord Publications and are available for purchase on their website, www.swordbooks.com.

Danny Orlis and Robin's Big Battle
© 2024 by Bernard Palmer
All rights reserved. First edition 1965.
Second edition 2024.

Scripture quotations from The Authorized (King James) Version. Rights in the Authorized Version in the United Kingdom are vested in the Crown. Reproduced by permission of the Crown's patentee, Cambridge University Press.

Cover image: Adobe Firefly

Character illustrations: John Ball

Editor: Charlene Miskimen

Aneko Press *Youth*

www.anekopress.com

Aneko Press, Life Sentence Publishing, and our logos are trademarks of Life Sentence Publishing, Inc.
203 E. Birch Street
P.O. Box 652
Abbotsford, WI 54405

JUVENILE FICTION / Religious / Christian / Action & Adventure

Paperback ISBN: 979-8-88936-024-7

eBook ISBN: 979-8-88936-025-4

10 9 8 7 6 5 4 3 2 1

Available where books are sold

CONTENTS

CHAPTER 1

EXCITEMENT AHEAD

The bleak winter sun pushed through the afternoon clouds, but only for a moment. Once more the soft, powdery snow began to sift downward to form a new white covering for the packed drifts of earlier snows. Jim Morgan noticed it as he hurried out of the school building and down the steps.

"Just a minute, Robin!" he called out, breaking into a run.

Robin Evans stopped and turned to face him. "Oh, it's you, Jim. I couldn't imagine who was calling me."

"I think we'd better have another committee meeting soon. There's not much time before the youth group's skiing retreat."

"Any time you and Edith can get together, I'll come," replied Robin.

He thought momentarily.

"How about meeting at the church half an hour before

the youth group leaders meeting tonight?" he asked. "We've got most of the planning done. Now all that's left is seeing that each one has done what he said he'd do."

"I've taken care of my responsibilities," Robin said, smiling. "And I've been wondering when you were going to call another meeting. I'll be there, Jim."

"Good. Why don't you call Edith and see if she can come."

"I'm sure she'd much rather hear from you. Do you know what she told me the other day? She said you're 'cute.'"

Jim Morgan's neck and face flushed crimson. "Aw–"

"And I think you are too. In a bashful sort of way."

"Lay off, will you? You know I don't like girls yet."

Her eyebrows arched. "Why, Jim. I'm crushed. I thought you liked me."

"I–I do," he stammered."

"But you just said you didn't."

He glanced at her helplessly. "Aw, you know what I mean."

Her laughter trilled in the still, cold air. They walked down the street for half a block or so before either of them spoke.

"I'm so excited about this ski retreat I can hardly wait for it," Robin said at last. "I think it's a wonderful idea."

"You can say that again."

"It's the best thing our youth group has ever done. I've had half a dozen kids come up and ask me if I could help them get in on it."

"The same thing's happened to me," Jim said. "I think we could get half the kids in school if we wanted to."

"We've got to call a halt somewhere, I suppose," Robin continued, "or we'll have such a big group we won't be able to feed them all or find a place for everybody to sleep. But as it is we're going to have a lot of unsaved girls and guys out there." Her attractive face grew serious. "That excites me more than the thought of learning to ski."

"That's what I've been thinking about. It really gives us a chance to challenge some of our friends for Christ." Unconsciously Jim lowered his voice. "We've really got to pray a lot about the retreat."

"And for Danny," Robin added. "He's going to be our speaker."

"If he hasn't got anything else going on that weekend," Jim replied.

"Haven't you asked him yet?"

"Couldn't. He hasn't been home."

"You've got to see him right away, Jim. If Danny can't be our speaker, it will ruin everything."

"He ought to be home tonight."

Danny Orlis did not arrive home before Jim had to go to the church, but he was there when the boy got home.

"Hi, Danny. I'm sure glad to see you."

"And just what've you been up to that you've got to see me so soon?"

Jim pulled up a footstool and sat down near the youthful pilot. Kay, Danny's wife, sat across from them.

"We've been planning a ski retreat during Christmas vacation, Danny."

"Hm. Sounds good."

"It's better than that. It's going to be great!" Excitement gleamed in Jim's eyes and sounded in his voice. "We've got a great place to go."

"Is it any place I know?"

"I think so. Have either you or Kay been out to Fleschman's Hill?" Jim asked.

"Oh, sure," Danny replied, "I remember it. We've been out there skiing a few times. It's the big hill west of town."

"That's right. It's the best ski hill around here. And, what's more, there are several cabins that we can use. Robin and her dad contacted the owners and got permission for us to use them."

"Sounds as though you've got everything under control." His gaze met Jim's. "At least as far as taking care of the kids and the skiing are concerned."

"We haven't forgotten the program, either." Jim leaned forward. "We've spent more time on the program than we have on anything else. We decided right from the first that we wanted this to be more than just a few days of skiing. We want it to count for something in the lives of all of us."

Danny and Kay nodded their agreement.

"You've got the right idea on that score," Danny said. "I'm all for having fun, but I think a youth group is missing the boat if it's all fun and there's no spiritual emphasis."

"That's what Robin said tonight when we were having our meeting," Jim went on. "We did a lot of debating, Danny. At first we thought that since we'd be having some unsaved kids along we ought to make the main thrust salvation. But then we decided it ought to be a missionary emphasis."

Kay nodded in approval. "I think you made the right decision. If the speaker is aware of the fact that some of his listeners aren't Christians, he can weave a strong salvation message into a missionary series. Don't you think so, Danny?"

"Of course. Who's going to speak for you, Jim?"

Jim eyed him inquisitively. "We've decided, but we haven't found out yet if he'll do it."

"You'd better get on the stick, Jim," Danny said. "Most of the men who would be good for a group like this are very busy."

"The guy we've picked out is busy, all right."

"Then you'd better get busy and ask him."

"That's what I'm trying to do."

Danny's eyes widened. "You mean you want me to speak to your group?"

"That's right," Jim replied. "We've all agreed on it."

Danny laughed.

"Will you do it?" Jim asked.

Danny's face was serious. "I don't know. Maybe I should make you beg me."

"Danny!" Kay scolded.

"I'll even do that, if it will help any," Jim said solemnly.

"It won't help a bit," Danny laughed. "I'll be glad to come."

The corners of Jim's mouth raised in a grin. "I told the rest of the committee that you'd do it." He turned toward Kay. "And I told them you'd be glad to come up and help us too, Kay."

She shook her head. "I wish I could do it, Jim. Honestly I do. But I have Kent and Jill to look after, and I wouldn't feel right about leaving them."

"That's easy. Bring them along."

Kay frowned and Danny shook his head. "Perhaps that would be all right some other time," he said, "but right now I don't feel that it would be wise. I think I'd better go alone this time."

Jim knew that it was useless for him to plead further. When Danny used that tone his mind was made up and there was no changing him.

"Okay," he said, "but we sure would like to have you both come."

"And I'd like to come too," Kay assured him. "Believe me, I would. Thank you, Jim, but not this time."

CHAPTER 2

JIM'S DECISION

Christmas came and went. And at last the time for the ski retreat arrived. Danny and Jim packed their gear, tied their skis on top of the car, and drove over to the church. Several carloads of excited, laughing guys and girls, together with George and Tina Olson, who had agreed to go along to serve as chaperons and to help with the cooking, were waiting.

While they were loading the cars two more girls joined them. At last Jim looked at his watch and turned to Danny and Mr. Olson. "It's already half an hour after the time we told everyone to be here," he said. "What do you think? Should we take off or wait a little longer?"

"Why don't you give them another five minutes, Jim?" Mr. Olson said, "Just in case someone else does want to go." They actually waited another ten minutes before leaving, but there was no one else.

"Okay, everybody!" Jim called out. "Let's pile in and get on the way."

Robin hadn't noticed that Linda Penner had been waiting in the front seat of Danny's car until everyone climbed in and settled. "Why, hello, Linda," she said. "I didn't know you were here."

"I wouldn't miss this trip for anything!"

"Neither would I."

"This is going to be great fun!" Linda exclaimed.

Robin took a long breath and sighed slowly. "I haven't seen you since school got out for Christmas vacation," she began. "Where've you been keeping yourself?"

Linda felt the color creep up into her cheeks. "I've had a good reason for not being in youth group," she said icily. "If that's what you're digging at me for."

Robin felt her own temper flare, and it was all she could do to keep from replying angrily to her friend.

"I've missed you at church and youth group," she acknowledged, "but that wasn't what I was talking about."

Linda shrugged her shoulders. "I've really been in a whirl since Christmas." She giggled. "There's been a party almost every night."

Robin was silent momentarily. "Didn't I see you riding with Jack Ross in his car the other evening?" she asked testingly.

Linda's face showed her surprise and embarrassment. She glanced quickly at Danny before turning to look at Robin once more.

"He just took me home a couple of nights ago," she

said offhandedly. "That's all. I wouldn't have ridden with him if it hadn't been so cold that I didn't want to walk."

Robin did not reply.

"And I can tell you this much," Linda went on loudly. "Even that's not going to happen again. I don't care what happens, I'm not going to be dating Jack Ross or anyone like him."

Robin looked as if she were about to speak, but she did not.

Linda, too, lapsed into silence, but her thoughts were racing. *What I said is true,* she told herself doggedly. She hadn't really had a date with Jack, even though she had been with him a few times lately in addition to riding home with him. But that was all over now. She was through with Jack. Positively. She wouldn't even ride with him anymore, let alone let him take her anywhere. She and Jack were through. Finished.

By the time they arrived at Fleschman's Hill and got situated in the cabins, it was too late for any skiing that day. They gathered in the main cabin to eat, then sitting around the fireplace, they drank hot chocolate and began singing some songs. Finally the time came for Danny to speak. He got to his feet and stood before the fireplace, his hands in his pockets. For a few minutes he joked with them and they all laughed uproariously. Then with skill that comes from practice, he changed the subject.

"I'm going to talk with you this evening about something that is very important for every Christian."

He paused to give time for his words to register. "We are all interested in the Lord's will for our lives. We want to do what He wants us to do."

As he spoke, an alert, expectant hush settled over the little group.

"However, we must remember that before we can be used by God, we must be usable. We must be living in such a way that He can use us. We must be walking so closely to Him that we can hear the whisper of the Holy Spirit when He speaks to us."

Jim Morgan leaned forward, his gaze transfixed on Danny. It was as though they were the only ones in the room at the moment.

"We often wonder what we can do for God," Danny went on, "but I want you to think about something. God is much more interested in what we are than He is in what we can do for Him. I know that this is the first service of our retreat. I didn't plan to ask anything particular of you tonight. But I feel that God would have me give you an opportunity to make a decision for Him."

His voice lowered. "Tonight I'm asking that you will stand to show that you want your life to be totally different than it has been – that you want to have a clean life that God can use – that you are ready and willing to do whatever He calls you to do."

Danny took a step closer to them. "This is not an easy decision I'm asking for, and I don't intend to press you. But if you mean business with God – if you really love

Him enough to trust yourself to Him without reservation – if you are willing with His help to do whatever He calls on you to do, I'd like to have you stand."

Almost before Danny quit speaking, Jim got to his feet. No one else followed his example and in a moment or two Danny finished the meeting.

The message had a quieting effect on everyone. The kids had been laughing and joking after dinner and into the song service, but when Danny finished, they were subdued and thoughtful. No one had asked them to be quiet, but they were, just the same.

Jim got an armful of logs and built up the fire in the fireplace. Then he sat down, cross-legged, before it, looking pensively into the flames. He scarcely moved when Danny came over to him.

"I was glad to see you make that decision, Jim," the young missionary pilot said in hushed tones. "I was thrilled and very proud of you."

Jim did not look up. "I–I don't know whether I can live up to it or not," he stammered.

"I can tell you the answer to that right now." Danny spoke confidently. "You can't live up to it, Jim. None of us can live up to a decision like that in our own strength. But the wonderful thing is that we don't have to live up to it alone. Christ has promised to live in us and through us to help us be what He wants us to be."

Jim moved uneasily for a moment, then sat quietly. When he spoke, it was with great emotion. "I–I'll sure need all the help I can get. That's certain." Slowly he turned until his gaze met Danny's. "You know, I've been thinking all these years that I've been living a consecrated life. I don't smoke or drink or swear or do a lot of things some of the guys my age are doing. But when I start to look into my life and see what it really is and how far short I've been falling of living the way I should, it makes me wonder why God would even bother to save someone like me."

Some of the other kids had stopped talking and listened to what was being said, but that didn't bother either Danny or Jim. The young missionary placed his hand reassuringly on Jim's shoulder. "You've come a long way, Jim, from the time you were saved. And you've made another big step forward now, just by seeing yourself as you really are and making a decision to turn your life over to God."

There was a long silence between them.

"What do you think I ought to do, Danny?" Jim asked at last. "Should I become a minister or go out to the mission field?"

Danny shook his head. "I wouldn't say that you necessarily ought to go to the mission field. That isn't the important thing right now."

Jim eyed him curiously. "It–it isn't?"

"I think that's where we, as young people, often make a big mistake," Danny continued. "We make a decision of consecration and right away we think that God wants us in the ministry or on the mission field. That might not be His plan for our lives at all."

Jim turned that over in his mind thoughtfully. "I always thought that's what consecration meant."

"Often that's what it does mean. But the important thing for you is to be in God's will. If He wants you to go to the mission field, then by all means that's what you ought to do. But He may want you as a pastor here in America or perhaps as a Christian business-man or a farmer or in one of the professions."

Jim's voice rose in his bewilderment. "But how–how will I know what God wants me to do?" he asked. By this time conversation in the big room ceased and the kids stood nearby, listening intently.

"Your chief concern is to be yielded to Him and His will, Jim," Danny explained. "If you are com-pletely yielded to Him, you won't have to worry about knowing what to do. He'll show you."

That night Jim lay on the top bunk staring up through the dark. There was a warmth in his heart he had never experienced before – a feeling of satis-faction and assurance. As Danny had said, it really didn't make any difference what he would be doing for the Lord. The thing that counted was to be in the Lord's will. What God had for him to do, he did not know; but of this he was sure: it was going to be something very special. It had to be.

Toward morning Jim finally drifted into sleep.

CHAPTER 3

TOM IS QUESTIONED

Jim had lain awake so long the night before that he was sleeping soundly when the others got up. He was the last to get out of bed. In fact, he would not have gotten up even then if Tom Channing had not stuck his head in the bedroom and called to him. "Come on, Jim. They're getting breakfast ready. If you don't hurry, you'll miss out on everything."

He shook the sleep from his head and swung his feet over the side of the cot. "I'll be right there."

Shivering, Jim grabbed his clothes and got dressed. The temperature had dropped considerably during the night and an inch or so of new snow had fallen. He looked out. Fortunately the wind had gone down and the overcast was clearing.

"Think it's going to snow any more today, Tom?" he asked.

Tom shook his head. "It won't snow any more. It

can't. It would ruin our skiing if it did." They got their coats and stepped out into the bracing winter air.

"Have you ever skied before, Jim?" Tom asked.

"Oh, sure. We used to do a lot of it back home on the Angle."

"Is it hard?"

"Naw. There's nothing to it."

Tom sighed deeply. "I've always wanted to learn to ski, but I've never even owned a pair of skis until now." He laughed nervously. "I've been wondering how I'd manage on them."

"You won't have any trouble. It's a cinch." They walked on in silence for a hundred yards or so.

"That was some message last night, wasn't it?" Jim asked, changing the subject.

Tom nodded. "I thought it was pretty good."

Perplexity showed in Jim's eyes. Tom had said what he had expected him to say, but there was a strange tone in his voice, as though Tom had some reservations about the service of the evening before.

"I thought it was the most challenging message I ever heard in my life," Jim went on. "The things Danny said got hold of me in a way they never have before."

"It was pretty good," Tom repeated.

"You know," Jim said, his earnest voice rising, "I'd always thought I was living a good Christian life because I didn't do the things the kids who aren't Christians do. But last night Danny showed us that

that's only half the story. I'd never before understood what it meant to live a consecrated life. Did you?"

"I said it was fine." Irritation sounded in Tom's voice.

"I've considered myself a consecrated Christian for a long time," Jim said, "but I don't believe I have ever honestly reached the point where I have been willing to turn my life over to God and let Him have complete and absolute control. I've always wanted to keep my hand on the wheel just a little in case God started to take me some place I didn't want to go."

Tom did not reply.

"I see now that's why I haven't had the victory in my Christian life that I should have. I hadn't been willing, until last night, to turn my whole life to Him and say, 'Lord, here I am. Do whatever You want to do with me.'"

His companion kicked a chunk of ice along the trail with his boot. Only a strange, haunted look in his dark eyes revealed his deeper thoughts. "I–I suppose there's some truth in what you're saying," he answered reluctantly.

Quizzically, Jim frowned at him. That didn't sound like Tom. That didn't sound like him at all. At the breakfast table, Tom, who usually laughed and joked as much as anyone, was remarkably quiet. He seemed to have his mind on something else, even when they finished eating and went out to ski.

Robin was standing near the gentle slopes that had been pointed out for the beginners. Tom saw her and headed her direction, a smile lighting his face. "Hi, Robin," he said. "I didn't expect to see you on this side. I thought I was the only untalented one in the place."

She smiled warmly. "I've only been on skis once before," she confessed frankly, "and that time I was positive I was going to break my neck!"

"I've never been on them," he said. "It looks as though we're partners."

"That's nice."

"What say we try it and break our necks together?"

She shuddered. "To tell you the truth, I don't like the sound of that, Tom."

"Neither do I." He laughed. "But as long as we're here, I guess we'd just as well get with it. We can learn to ski together – or should I say we can try to learn to ski?"

"That's probably closer to the truth."

He stood his own skis against a big tree. "Come over here and I'll see if I can help you put yours on."

She stepped into them, and he knelt to fasten them in place. Robin looked down, watching him. "What did you think of Danny's message last night?"

There was a brief silence. For an instant Tom stopped what he was doing. Robin repeated her question and he looked up quickly. "Oh, I guess it was all right," he said with affected carelessness. "If you happen to like that type of talk. I suppose you could even say that it was sort of challenging."

Her face was even more serious than it had been

a moment before. "I couldn't get it out of my mind last night," she admitted. "To tell you the truth, I don't think I slept more than two or three hours."

Tom scowled. "Well, frankly, I thought Danny was being a little too hard on us. After all, everybody can't be a preacher or go out to the mission field. Somebody's got to stay at home and be business-men or farmers or lawyers and doctors. We can't all become preachers."

The anger in his voice was something of a surprise to him. He had heard other calls for full-time Christian service – many of them. What was there about this one that made him so angry? Or was God really talk-ing to him and he didn't want to listen? Was that why he was so disturbed? He felt his heartbeat quicken.

He forced himself to finish buckling on Robin's skis, then got into his own. His hands were trembling as he fastened the straps, but not from the cold.

They made their way over to the beginners' slope together. They compared the little instruction which they had had in the handling of skis. At least the theo-ries of the sport were not entirely foreign to them. But actually skiing was something else again. Tom thrust his poles into the snow timorously and pushed himself forward a few feet. He almost lost his balance.

"I almost went that time." he exclaimed.

Robin tried it too, with no better results. "I don't know whether I'll ever have the courage to learn to ski or not," she said, stopping to look about uneasily.

"I think it'll be fun," Tom said, getting balanced and ready to try again.

"So do I, if I can ever get the hang of it," Robin replied.

Tom grinned at her. "When Danny explained how to ski it sounded easy," he said. "And when I watch the rest of them scoot down the hill it looks easy. I'll have to say that. It makes me think that all I have to do is give myself a shove and I'll be off – that there's nothing to it."

"It's sort of like what Danny was saying about living a Christian life," she said. "Just hearing it makes it sound so attractive and so–so easy, but–"

Tom finished the sentence for her. "But when you start to put it into practice it's an entirely different thing."

There was a long, tense silence.

"Tell me, Tom," Robin continued, "how did the message affect you?"

His gaze met hers. "What did it mean to you?" he countered.

She took a long, deep breath.

"Well, it – well, I just don't know for sure how to answer that. Sometimes I think it's wonderful and shows the only way in the world for a young Christian to live. But then again–" Her voice trailed off.

"To tell you the truth," Tom said, "I was disappointed. It seems to me that every time Danny talks to us, he has to harp on going out to the mission field. But as I said a minute ago, I can't go along with that. I don't believe God calls everybody."

Robin did not answer him.

CHAPTER 4

THE ACCIDENT

The following morning Tom, Jim, and some of the other guys were standing outside the boys' cabin with Mr. Olson, their sponsor, looking up at slate-gray clouds.

"What do you think, Danny?" George Olson asked, "Is it going to snow?"

Danny shook his head. "I hardly think so," he answered, "But it's difficult to tell. At this time of year we could get a real blizzard."

Tom spoke up. "I heard the weather forecast a few minutes ago. It said cloudy skies with possible snow flurries. It doesn't sound to me as though it's going to get too bad."

Mr. Olson agreed. "The clouds don't look too bad to me, to tell you the truth. They don't look thick or dark enough to give us much snow."

The boys brightened noticeably. "Then it's all right

for us to go skiing again today instead of packing up right away and leaving for home?"

Danny looked over at the sponsor. "What do you think, George?"

Mr. Olson noted the time. "I think perhaps we'd better get packed up so we can leave in a hurry if we need to. But I don't think there's any particular need for us to leave yet. All that really matters is that we get back by dark unless it does start to storm."

They hurried back to their cabins and packed their gear and ate a hurried lunch before going out on their skis. Tom, though he had been gaining skill rapidly in the short time they had been skiing, still went over to the beginners' slope. Jim saw him and called to him.

"Come on over here, Tom. It's a lot more fun."

Tom waved his hand. "Not me. I'll take my skiing over here where I belong. I don't want to break my neck just yet."

He did feel a bit safer on the beginners' side of the hill, but that wasn't the only reason he insisted on skiing there. He didn't want to be with the others – not just now, at any rate. He wanted to be alone where he could think.

Robin was already there, trying awkwardly to negotiate the slope. Tom surveyed the area ahead. The stretch directly in front of him was gentle enough, but beyond Robin and to the right, the hill fell away rapidly. "Hey, Robin!" he called out. "Let's try it over there."

"Not me!" she retorted. "This is steep enough to interest me without going anywhere else."

Tom gave himself a shove with his poles and began to move forward. He scooted past Robin, gathering speed, and reached the steeper slope. "This is great!" he sang out. "You ought to try it, Robin!"

The speed was exhilarating. The wind stung his face as he went faster and faster. Just when the excitement turned to panic he did not know. Perhaps it was when he saw the ground rushing under him, or the trees flying past on either side. But panic he did.

He had to turn at the bottom of the hill. There was no other way! But how? His mind blanked. Everything Danny and the others had taught him about skiing vanished from his thoughts.

Frantically, Tom threw himself into the snow. There was a dull, crunching sound. Fire stabbed through his left leg as he rolled and tumbled in the snow. Then he lay motionless at the bottom of the slope. He felt dizzy and far away. For the space of a minute or more he did not know where he was or what he had been doing. He blinked, opened his eyes, and forced them into focus. Slowly he realized that he had fallen and was lying on his back in the snow.

That was all. He was vaguely aware of the fact that he hurt, but it wasn't localized enough for him to know where. With effort he drew an arm up under him and tried to raise himself. As he moved, great shooting pains seized his thigh. Icy sweat covered his face and a violent trembling seized him. An agonizing groan escaped his lips as he settled back in the snow. Once more dizziness and nausea gripped him. His fists clenched as he fought against the pain.

He was still feeling the viselike hold of the pain when Robin came hurrying down to him. "Tom!" she cried, "are you all right?"

He turned a little to look up into her frightened eyes. He forced himself to speak. "I'm not sure. I–I think there's something wrong with my leg," he stammered. "It sure does hurt like everything."

Robin's face became pale as she saw that his leg was doubled grotesquely under him.

Tom started to speak, but the words choked off and he grimaced involuntarily.

Robin reached out and touched his leg hesitantly. "It–it looks as though it must be–" She could not put her thoughts into words.

"I think my leg's broken," Tom said, his gaze meeting hers. "Do you think you can get back to where the others are skiing and–and tell Danny what a stupid, idiotic thing I did?"

She stood quickly and looked around. They had been so involved with the accident that neither of them had noticed the snow before that very moment. Now it seemed as though the accident had somehow triggered the wind and snow. Great billowing clouds of wet snow swirled about them, choking away their breath and blotting out the trees and even the nearest landmarks at times.

"I–I think I can find the cabins," Robin said hesitantly.

Tom saw the indecision in her manner – and the stark fright in her eyes. She was afraid to go off into the storm alone to try to find the cabins. And he did not blame her.

"The way this storm is," he said, trying to sound casual and unafraid himself, "maybe it would be better if we stay together."

Robin looked about helplessly. "But we'll have to stay here," she protested. "You can't walk with your leg the way it is."

"It doesn't hurt quite so bad now," Tom said, managing a weak smile, trying to be reassuring. "Maybe if you can help me to my feet, I'll be able to walk."

He took hold of her arm and tried to raise himself, managing all right until he started to move the injured leg. Pain slammed him to the ground. It was a minute or two before he could speak.

"It's no use," he said. "I can't do it."

"I'll go, Tom," Robin said firmly.

He held on to her coat sleeve. "I hate to see you go off alone, Robin," he told her. "The way it's snowing it's going to be tough even finding the cabins."

"Don't worry about me," she spoke quickly. "God will take care of me." With that she turned away from him, stumbling through the drifts. New snow swirled about her until she had only the vaguest idea of her directions. But she could not allow that to stop her. Every moment's delay could make things that much worse – could make it that much harder for her to find the cabins – could make it that much worse for Tom.

Robin scrambled up the slope in what she thought was the direction of the cabins. The snow and wind snatched her breath, leaving her gasping as she drove herself forward, and the cold penetrated her parka to the very depths of her bones. She could not stop. She did not dare.

She should have been going up the wide clearing that made the ski run, but Robin hadn't been walking more than three or four minutes when she stubbed her toe on a fallen tree and sprawled, headlong, into the snow. It pushed up into her sleeves and around her face.

Robin lay there, motionless for an instant, lacking the strength to get to her feet. She wanted to stay there. How she wanted to. But she had to go on! Wearily, Robin got to her feet and started forward once more. She was still going uphill, or so it seemed. All she had to do was go to the first level stretch and turn toward the right. The cabins ought to be in that direction, not too far away.

Robin stopped suddenly and looked around. The unfamiliarity struck her and fear swept through her in a great surging wave.

She was lost!

CHAPTER 5

THE SEARCH

The rest of the skiers had come back to the cabins when the first few snowflakes began to filter down. Danny and Mr. and Mrs. Olson directed the kids as they loaded their gear into the cars.

"We've got to move as quickly as we can," Danny said. "This storm looks as though it could be a bad one, and we've got quite a distance to drive. We don't want to get stranded out here."

Mrs. Olson looked about, concern growing in her eyes. "Have you seen Robin around anywhere?"

Danny's forehead furrowed. "Robin Evans?" he echoed. "Isn't she here?"

"I don't think so. I haven't been able to locate her, and her things are still in the cabin," replied Mrs. Olson.

"Are you sure?" George Olson demanded.

"I just came from there."

"That isn't like Robin," Danny said. "She's not the

kind of a girl to go off somewhere without letting someone know."

At that moment Jim Morgan came rushing up to them. "Hey," he called out, "where's Tom Channing?"

Danny glanced back toward the cabin. "He ought to be around here someplace. I saw him just a short while ago."

"I saw him not long ago, too," Jim went on. "But he's not here now. His stuff is still in the middle of the floor where he left it after he packed up."

"That is strange," Mrs. Olson said. "You don't suppose they went off somewhere together, do you?"

Danny shook his head. "I suppose they could have, but I can scarcely believe they did. That's not like either Tom or Robin. They're about the most reliable kids we have."

Jim's eyes widened. "Do you suppose something happened to them?" he asked. "I saw them over on the beginners' slope not long ago."

Danny's voice revealed his tenseness. "We'll have to see." He turned to Mr. Olson. "Don't you think we ought to have two of the cars go back to town to beat the storm?"

The youth group's sponsor shook his head. "I don't think so. It's snowing harder all the time. I don't think we ought to separate."

"Probably not," Danny answered, his concern reflected on his face. "We don't want to get anyone caught out on the highway in a blizzard. Then too, we may need all the help we can get to find Robin and Tom."

"What do you plan to do?" George Olson asked.

"First, I think I'll take Jim and go out to see if we can find them. He's had some experience in the woods."

"Finding them's not going to be too easy in this storm. The way it looks to me, we're going to have a full-fledged blizzard before too long."

Danny called Boyd Patterson over to them and told him what they were going to do. "You're one of the older guys, Boyd," he said guardedly, "so I'm going to have to depend on you to help Mr. and Mrs. Olson keep the kids busy doing something while Jim and I are gone."

"Got any ideas?" Boyd asked.

"You can have them cut firewood and carry it into the cabins and get some snow melted for water," Danny said. "That ought to keep them busy for quite a while. Stay near the cabins."

Boyd lowered his voice. "Do you think we might be snowed in here?"

"Not necessarily," Danny replied. "I don't know. Right now our chief concern is to get everybody busy and keep them so busy they won't have a chance to think about Tom and Robin or the fact that we might be snowed in."

The boy nodded in understanding. "You can count on me, Danny."

"I knew I could." Danny laid a hand on his shoulder. "Mr. Olson said he wants to get everybody together for prayer first. As soon as that's finished, get the kids to work and see that they're kept busy as long as possible."

"Do you think it will take long to find them?"

Danny's usually happy eyes looked troubled. "It's not going to be easy, Boyd," he said frankly. "This country is all heavily wooded. And with the snow and wind keeping visibility to zero the going will be very slow."

"We'll be praying for you."

"Thanks."

* * *

The frigid winter wind snarled ominously across the hillside. It was a savage wind that did not ease off, crackling through the trees and whipping the new-fallen snow into huge choking clouds that enveloped Danny and Jim like opaque white shrouds driving the snow and cold into the folds of their parkas. The gusts left them breathless, but still they fought their way forward, relentlessly.

Danny paused and half turned toward his companion, hunching his back against the fierce wind. "Jim!" he yelled, "are you all right?"

"I think so!" It was a great effort even to speak. "How long will we look for them, Danny?"

For a brief instant snow hid them from one another. Jim repeated his question. This time Danny straightened deliberately. "We're not going to quit until we find them!"

For the space of a few heartbeats his gaze searched the curtain of white that encircled them. Then grimly he pushed forward with Jim at his heels. Together they floundered through the growing drifts.

But why? Danny asked himself. *Why keep battling helplessly against the storm? Why keep looking for Tom and Robin when the search seems so hopeless?* Neither he nor Jim could see anything. They could see nothing at all! Nothing! They were just roaming aimlessly about in the cold and snow. *Why keep doing it? Why?* The question pounded through his very being.

Every moment they were moving farther and farther from the cabin. Every moment it was going to be that much more difficult for them to find their way back. But how could they stop when they knew that Tom and Robin were lost somewhere in the forest nearby? When to stop might well mean that they were giving up their young friends to death?

Danny and Jim were moving forward slowly with great effort. They strained to see a few feet ahead. Time seemed to stand still. Danny reckoned that they had crossed the broad plateau and had come down the first steep ski run. Suddenly, the wind ceased and the snow began to settle. Jim caught hold of Danny's arm.

"Looks as though it–" The words caught in his throat. "Danny!" he shouted. "Look over there!" A dark form, half covered by snow, lay on the slope a short distance to their right.

"It's Tom!" Danny cried, forcing forward through the snow. He reached the injured boy shortly before Jim and knelt beside him. "Tom! Are you all right?"

Tom fought against it, but a faint groan escaped between clenched teeth. "I–I'm all right," he managed bravely, "but where's Robin?" Fear glazed his eyes and his voice sounded taut with pain.

"Wasn't she with you?" Danny demanded.

Tom's voice caught. "Sh–she left a little while ago. She went for help. I–I thought she brought you to find me."

It was an instant or two before Danny could bring himself to speak. "We haven't seen her." He hoped his voice sounded more confident than he felt. "She'll probably be back at the cabin when we get there."

"I didn't want her to leave," said Tom. "She was so scared to go off alone that I–I didn't want her to leave, but she did anyway."

Danny examined Tom with care, frowning as he saw the boy's leg. "Looks to me as though you've got a break here, Tom," he said.

The injured boy nodded. "I figured it was broken."

He caught his breath as the pain stabbed savagely through him.

Danny glanced in Jim's direction. "Stay here with Tom. I'm going to get a couple of branches for a splint."

He was back shortly and bound the splints carefully along Tom's injured leg to keep the broken bone in place as much as possible. At last he straightened.

"You stay here with Tom, Jim," he said. "I think I'd better go back and get the others."

"But you can't do that, Danny!" Tom protested. "You'll never be able to find us again."

"I have a good idea of distances and direction now, and I can follow my tracks back here," Danny assured him, "if I hurry before they get filled in."

With that he turned and started up the slope in the direction from which they had just come. For several minutes Jim huddled close to Tom, saying little. Tom grimaced with pain and looked away to hide the beginning tears in his eyes.

"Danny'll be back before you know it, Tom," Jim said. "And after he gets here with the guys, we won't be long in carrying you up to the cabin where it's warm."

"R–Robin!" Tom's voice quavered. "We've got to find her!"

"We'll find her. We'll find her." Numbly Jim bowed his head and began to pray.

* * *

Danny led the boys to the place where Tom was lying injured. Darkness was already beginning to close in about them. As they approached, Jim jumped to his feet.

"I'm sure glad to see you guys!" he shouted. "I thought you'd never get back!"

Danny knelt beside Tom. "I'd have been back sooner,

but I found Robin wandering around in the snow about halfway between here and the cabins," he said.

Tom's face brightened. "You found her?"

"That's right."

"Thank God!" Tom reached out and grasped Danny by the sleeve. "Is–is she all right?"

"She's suffering from exhaustion and shock," he said, "and her cheeks and fingers are frostbitten, but I don't think there's any question that she's going to be all right."

Tom sighed deeply. "I've been praying that she'd be found." A shudder ran through his body. "Like I told you, Danny, I tried to get her to stay here. But she wouldn't do it. She said she had to go and try to find help."

"We can do our talking when we get back to the cabin where it's warm." Danny turned to the boys who had come with him. "All right, guys, bring the stretcher and let's get on the way. If it gets dark before we get to the cabins, our job'll be just that much harder."

Taking the stretcher which they had found among the first aid supplies, they placed it close to Tom. Jim, Boyd, and Danny carefully lifted Tom onto it. Four of the boys picked up the stretcher and began the struggle up the ski slope in the direction of the cabins. The going was slow, and it was half an hour or more before they finally reached the buildings. As Danny opened the door to go inside, one of the girls hurried over to him, her face alert with fear.

"Danny!" she gasped. "We've got to do something! Robin's awfully sick!"

CHAPTER 6

THE RESCUE

While the boys carried Tom into the cabin and transferred him from the stretcher to a bed near the stove, Danny went into the next room where Robin had been put to bed. Her cheeks were flushed, and she was trembling convulsively. Mrs. Olson was bending over her.

Danny knelt beside the bed. "How is she?" he asked in a tense whisper.

At the sound of his voice, Robin opened her eyes and smiled faintly. "I–I'm all right."

He returned her smile. "Of course you're all right." He pulled the blanket a bit higher under her chin and tucked it in. "Are you getting warm yet?" he asked.

"I–I don't know," she managed. "I haven't quit shaking long enough to find out. I've never been so cold in all my life."

There was a brief silence. Then Robin stiffened

suddenly, as though she just remembered. "Tom!" she gasped, her voice catching. "Is he all right?"

Danny nodded. "He's going to be all right," he said. "He's got a broken leg, but I'm sure there's nothing more serious than that wrong with him."

She sighed. "God answered our prayers," she whispered.

"He certainly did. For both of you."

"I–I thought I could find the cabin," Robin began, but her voice trailed off wearily to a whisper. "But the snow was blowing so much I couldn't see anything and–and it was so awfully cold."

Danny got to his feet. "I think you've talked enough for now, Robin. You'd better close your eyes and try to get some sleep."

She did not protest.

Mrs. Olson followed Danny into the other room and closed the door behind them. "What do you think about her, Danny?" she asked, her face lined with concern.

"She's in shock now. She was pretty frightened and had quite an exposure to the blizzard. That's why she's shivering so much."

"That's what I thought," she answered in a low voice. "What bothers me the most is that she seems to be getting worse all the time."

He nodded.

"I think we must get her to a doctor, Danny. She's got a fever and her temperature is still going up. As cold as she was, she might be getting pneumonia."

"I'll take a look at Tom and see how he is," the young pilot said. "Then we'll decide what's best to do."

Tom was also in shock. Perhaps even worse than Robin. He was trembling so much that the bed shook with him. He lay there, restless with pain, his eyes closed.

"Tom," Danny said.

At the sound of his name, the injured boy opened his eyes. His lips parted, but he made no sound.

Mr. Olson came up just then and put another heavy comforter on him. Then he motioned Danny to one side. "What are we going to do, Danny?" he whispered.

"I think I'd better get to the nearest farmhouse with a landline and phone for help."

"I'll go with you."

The pilot shook his head. "I don't know how long I'll be gone, George. I don't believe it's wise for both of us to leave your wife here alone with the kids. You stay and look after things on this end. I'll go and get help."

Mr. Olson nodded. "I suppose that is best. We'll be praying for you."

Danny put on his parka once more and went out into the frigid night. It would be useless to try to take a car with the snow drifting the way it was. It would be far better to go on skis. The wind was still blowing, but the snow fell lightly with only occasional gusts. Although there was no moonlight, the whiteness of the ground contrasted the darker areas of the trees and gave Danny confidence for moving in the dark.

He moved off with certainty in the direction of the nearest farmstead. He had been in this area skiing and hunting a few times before and remembered seeing the farm. Though he did not know the areas as well as he knew the Northwest Angle back home, he had to trust his knowledge of it now. With a shove of his ski poles he began to pick up speed.

When the door closed behind Danny, Mr. Olson called the kids together in the big living room where Tom was lying on the daybed. "I know that most of you are disturbed by what has happened," he began, his voice calm and free of emotion. "It has been disturbing to all of us. But we can thank God that we were able to find Tom and Robin and get them back here where it's warm."

"What about getting home?" someone asked. "That's what I'd like to know."

"Danny's on his way to get help now," replied Mr. Olson.

Boyd Patterson broke in quickly. "I suppose you've already thought of it, Mr. Olson, but don't you think we ought to be praying for Danny – that he'll get through safely, and that Robin and Tom will be all right?"

George Olson smiled. "I was just coming to that, Boyd. Would you like to pray first, after I read a portion of Scripture?"

The guys and girls stood quietly while Mr. Olson read from one of the Psalms. Then they all bowed their heads. Boyd was the first to pray. Linda was second, and then Jim. Then following one another, each young person who knew the Lord took a turn.

Mr. Olson closed. "Father, we thank You for the wonderful way You have guided and led us during these difficult hours. We thank You for being with us, for watching over us and keeping us from harm during this storm. Now, we pray that You will keep Your loving hand on Robin and Tom and on Danny as he's on his way to get help–"

They had been praying for almost an hour, but no one in the cabin realized that it had been more than just a few minutes. A sense of calmness and peace settled over them.

* * *

Danny cut diagonally across the pasture and skied down the narrow road to the nearest farmhouse. Each breath – each movement – was a prayer.

"Oh, God, please, may they be home," he prayed. "Please, may they be home!"

They were! A light flickered invitingly in the living room window. New strength surged through Danny as he thrust his ski poles into the snow and shoved himself forward to the doorway.

* * *

Kay Orlis had expected Danny and the young people by dark that evening, but she had not yet begun to get concerned about them when he called from the farmer's house. Hurriedly he began explaining what had happened. She broke in excitedly. "Tom and Robin aren't seriously hurt, are they?"

"They're in shock, Kay," he explained. "I think that's the most pressing problem right now. It seems serious enough to be sure that we don't waste any time in getting medical help for them. I'd like you to call the doctor, tell him the situation and where we are. He can take care of contacting the highway department for a snowplow and getting the emergency unit."

Kent Gilbert had heard the phone ring and came out of his room to stand beside Kay. When she hung up, he turned to her. "What's wrong, Kay? Who was it?"

Without answering she dialed the doctor. As soon as she talked with him, she would have to call Mr. and Mrs. Channing and Mr. and Mrs. Evans. That was going to be the most difficult part, telling them. In spite of the fact that her voice was calm as she talked to the doctor, her hands were shaking.

* * *

It was after midnight when the emergency unit returned to Fairview with Tom and Robin.

Two hours later, Danny and the young people also

returned. Kay was waiting at the hospital with Tom's and Robin's parents when Danny arrived.

He hurried up to them. "How are they?" he asked.

"We don't know yet," Mrs. Channing said, concern showing in her face. "The doctor hasn't told us anything specific yet. Just that they're treating him for shock."

Mrs. Evans broke in quickly. "That's what they told us about Robin too," she said. Controlled anger sounded in her voice. "We should have known better than to let them go off on a dangerous trip like this in the wintertime." Tears welled up in her eyes. "We should have known that something terrible would happen."

Her husband put his arm around her shoulder. "Now, my dear. It doesn't do any good to talk that way."

"But it's true! I didn't want to let her go. Skiing is so dangerous! I didn't want her to even learn to ski."

Mrs. Evans did not criticize Danny or the Olsons directly, but the implication was clear.

"Robin has been going skating and tobogganing every winter since she's been old enough to know how," Mr. Evans countered. "Nothing like this has ever happened before. It's just one of those things."

"I know." She dried her eyes. "But if something happens to her, I–I'll never forgive myself for letting her go. I'll just *never* forgive myself."

Mrs. Channing nodded in agreement. "I know exactly how you feel. I can tell you this much. Tom's never going skiing again. That's certain!"

CHAPTER 7

JACK CORNERS KENT

With all the excitement around the Orlis home brought on by the skiing accident, no one paid much attention to Kent Gilbert for several days. He lingered at home as late as he dared in the morning, allowing himself just enough time to get to school before the last bell made him tardy. Then he ran as hard as he could run, cutting through alleys and across vacant lots. On the way home he took the shortest route, avoiding everyone he could.

Jack Ross wanted to talk to him. He sent word by one of the guys that Kent was to meet him at the snack shop right after school, but Kent did not go. Instead he headed in the opposite direction.

That was one thing that wasn't going to happen. He wasn't *ever* going to get into Jack's car again or even stop and talk to the guy if he could help it. He had already had enough of Jack. He wasn't going to get involved with Jack in any kind of a crooked deal again. He wasn't going to let Jack fool around and get him caught stealing something and risk being sent to jail.

For several days Kent was successful in avoiding the older boy. However, Jack kept a close watch and toward the end of the week, he caught Kent coming out of an alley. He drove up in his car and squealed to a stop in front of him.

"Hi, Kent," Jack said, a grin spreading across his face.

Kent did not answer him.

"I've been lookin' all over for you, Kent. Where've you been?"

The younger boy swallowed hard, but he held his ground. "I haven't been lookin' for you."

Jack continued watching Kent, a smirk accentuating his remark. "It's cold standin' out there," he said. "Come on. Hop in."

Still Kent did not move.

Jack scowled and raised his voice. "I said hop in," he ordered angrily. "You and I have got some things to talk about."

"No." Kent shook his head defensively. "There's no use askin' me. I–I'm not ridin' with you anymore."

The Ross boy smirked. "Who's goin' to know it if you go for a little ride with me?" he asked. "We'll take her out on the highway and see how fast she'll go. How about it?"

No answer.

"One of these days when we're somewhere where

the cops won't see us, I might even let you drive. You'd like that, wouldn't you?"

Kent's heart was hammering against his rib cage as he looked about, fearfully. "I–I–"

"Listen, Gilbert," Jack continued ominously, "I said I've got to talk to you and that's exactly what I mean. Come on and get in before I come around there and put you in!"

Reluctantly Kent moved to the car. Jack leaned over and jerked open the door. Kent got in beside him.

"There," Jack said. "That's better. That's much better."

Kent slid down in the seat until he could not be seen as Jack drove up Main Street.

"What's the deal, Kent?" Jack demanded. "Scared?"

Kent's mouth twitched nervously, but defiance edged his voice. "Scared?" he echoed. "What's there to be scared of?"

"I don't know." They left town and drove north on a snow-packed country road. "I thought maybe you were getting spooked by those stories in the news."

Kent twisted in the seat to stare at Jack. "What if I have been?"

"You wouldn't let a little thing like that scare you, now would you?"

"Don't tell me it didn't shake you up to read that the chief of police has put on an extra cop just to catch us." Kent's voice broke, "I tell you, Jack, they're goin' to get us!"

Jack laughed loudly. "They're not goin' to catch us unless we get cold feet and give ourselves away."

"What do you mean?"

"All we've got to do is keep our mouths shut and act as though nothing's happened. We didn't leave any clues. They haven't got a thing on any of us."

Kent relaxed slightly. "Are you sure about that?"

"Sure about it?" Jack echoed. "I'm positive. I told you I didn't jump into this deal. I got a lot of help from Riley, and he knows what he's doin'."

Kent's eyes narrowed. "Who's he?"

"He's the guy who's been buyin' the stuff." Jack checked himself. "Only don't say anything to any of the other guys about it. He doesn't want anyone else to know he's got anything to do with us."

"What makes you think he can help us?" Kent asked. "Keep away from the cops, I mean."

"He used to be in on a big deal in Chicago before he came out here," Jack said. "He knows what he's doin'. And when he says he knows how to keep us from havin' trouble with the cops, he knows how. That's all there is to it." Jack paused. "He spent hours and hours helping me work out all the details so we won't get caught." He laughed again. "So, you see, we haven't got a thing to worry about."

"Maybe you're right," the younger boy said reluctantly.

"Of course I'm right. It only stands to reason, Kent. If they had anything on us, we'd have been picked up a week ago."

As Jack talked, Kent's fear seemed to ease a little.

"I talked with Riley again last night, though,"

Jack went on. "And he thinks we ought to lay off for a while. He said we ought to let the town go back to sleep before we hit 'em again."

Kent sighed his relief. "I think that's a good idea. A real good idea. There's no need in gettin' everybody stirred up about us any more than they are already."

"Riley said I ought to talk to the rest of you guys and tell you not to worry, that nothing's going to happen. All we've got to do is lay low and we'll be okay."

Kent grinned. He felt better already just knowing that Jack wasn't going to try to get him to go out and steal anything for a while. He felt a great deal better. Jack wasn't such a bad guy, after all.

"Riley had to go down to the Twin Cities or Duluth or somewhere," Jack said. "He told me that he'd come back when he thought it was safe for us to go to work again."

The words stabbed deeply into Kent's heart. "You– you mean you're planning on doing it again? After all that's happened?"

"You sure don't think we're goin' to quit now, do you?" Jack demanded. "Why, we're just gettin' started. We've got a great thing goin' for us that'll make us all a lot of money. Just you wait! You haven't seen anything yet."

Suddenly Kent felt sick and weak inside. Jack wasn't going to quit. He was going to keep going on and on until they were all arrested. And the worst of it was that he couldn't get out of it, even if he wanted to. Jack and this Riley character wouldn't let him. He was trapped. Trapped!

CHAPTER 8

TOM'S CONFLICT

The third day that Tom was in the hospital the doctor took his leg out of traction, and Tom went to surgery to have the broken bone set and pinned. Robin, who was only treated for shock and exposure, was able to be up and around most of the time after the first day. Whenever she had the opportunity, she came into Tom's room to talk with him.

"Think you're going to be in here long, Tom?" she asked one afternoon.

He shrugged his shoulders. "Search me. I asked the doctor about it this morning and all he did was laugh as though I'd just told him a good joke."

She sat down in the chair beside the bed and crossed her legs. "I think I'll be going home today."

"So soon?" Tom asked.

"It doesn't seem so soon to me," she replied. "It seems as though I've been here for ages and ages."

"It's going to make the time go a lot slower for me after you're gone," he said. "I can tell you that much."

There was a short silence. "I'll be back to see you, Tom. I'm not sure whether they're going to let me go to school right away or not."

"Come any time," he said, grinning crookedly. "I think I'll be here."

She leaned back in the chair and closed her eyes momentarily.

"We can sure thank the Lord for the way everything turned out, can't we, Robin?" Tom said at last. "You know, we both could have frozen to death."

She sat up straight, her face pensive. "It makes us realize how much we owe Him, doesn't it?" she asked.

Tom raised himself on one elbow. "That's something that's been bothering me a great deal lately," he said. "The Lord has been so good to me. He has given me health, good parents, good schools – He even sent His Son to die on the cross so that I could be saved. But what am I willing to do for Him?"

Robin's voice faltered. "I've hardly been able to sleep the last two or three nights," she answered, "just for thinking about that and the things Danny said at the retreat."

"Me too."

"We aren't necessarily obligated as Christians to become missionaries or ministers or full-time Christian workers just because we've consecrated our lives to Christ," Robin went on. "He may have some other vocation for us. But we are obligated to give our very best to Christ and to turn every facet of our lives over to His direction."

Tom nodded seriously. "That's the thing I've been wrestling with," he said. "I first thought that consecration meant full-time Christian service, and it bugged me a little. But now I see that the important thing is for us to do what God wants us to do and to be what He wants us to be. He may want us in Alaska or Japan or Africa witnessing to people who have never heard of the Lord Jesus Christ. And, of course, if He calls us in one of those directions, then to remain in His will we have to go."

Robin's lips trembled slightly, and it was only with some difficulty that she was able to speak.

"That's what I'm afraid of," she said, her voice almost a whisper. "I'm afraid God will call me to some far-off place like that. And–and if He did, it would almost kill my mother and dad."

Tom lay back on the bed and was silent.

"My dad was in to see me a little while this morning," Tom said at last. "All he could talk about was the business and how glad he'll be when I'm out of high school and college so I can come home into the firm with him. You know, Robin, I don't know what he'd do if I didn't do something like that. It would really be rough on him."

It was some time before he continued. "I know how Dad feels and, to tell you the truth, I'd sort of like to go into business with him. But Danny talks as though every Christian has an obligation to turn his life over to Christ." Tom sighed slowly. "You sort of get the idea when Danny's talking that it's so easy to turn one's life to Jesus. All a person has to do is to let Christ have His will in our lives and all our troubles will be solved, as easy as that."

But Robin did not agree with him. "I don't think that's what Danny meant, Tom. I think he meant that when we turn our lives completely over to Christ, we will have access to all the help and strength we need to solve the problems that come our way."

"I suppose you're right." He lowered his voice. "Robin, I know you probably feel the same way as I do. I love the Lord and–and I want Him to have complete and absolute control of my life. I want to serve Him wherever He wants me to. But I love my parents too. And I don't want to go against their wishes."

Robin moistened her lips with the tip of her tongue. "Whenever I've said anything at home about becoming a missionary or anything like that, my mother used to quote the verse to me that children are to obey their parents."

Tom's jaw was set firmly. "I've been thinking a lot about that verse too. Then there's the part in the Bible where the man told Jesus he wanted to serve Him, but first he wanted to go home and bury his father. Jesus told him, *Let the dead bury their dead.* And in another place He told some people that whoever did not love the Lord more than their father or mother, did not love Him at all."

Tom took a long, deep breath. "I've been praying about it a lot," he confided, "but I sure haven't been able to come up with an answer yet."

* * *

Robin's doctor discharged her from the hospital that afternoon. While her mother waited for her, she went into Tom's room to say goodbye. He saw that she had put aside her robe for her street clothes.

"Now," he said, "where do you think you're going?"

"Hi," she retorted, smiling brightly.

"Don't tell me they're finally getting tired of having you around here."

"That's what they said. They can't stand me anymore, so they decided to let me go home." She grew serious. "I had to come in and say goodbye before I left. Mom's waiting for me in the hall."

Tom's angular face clouded. "Wow, are you lucky!" he exclaimed.

She came over to the bed. "I am sorry you have to stay, Tom. I think they'll be letting you out in a few days too."

"The doctor finally told me that I would get to leave sometime next week," he replied, "but I thought maybe you'd be around to come in and keep me company."

"I'm not going to get to go to school for a few days

at least," she said. "I'll see if I can get our assignments Monday and come up and study with you."

"Great. We can cry on each other's shoulders over all the work we've got to make up."

"It's a date."

After Robin had gone, Tom lay back on the pillow and closed his eyes. It hadn't been too pleasant staying in the hospital, but it was going to be a lot worse having to stay there now that Robin was gone. Just knowing she was down the hall had helped, and when she could come in and see him once in a while, he almost forgot that he had a broken leg and was flat on his back. He took a deep breath and let the air out slowly.

If only I could leave the hospital now! he thought. The doctor had said he could get out next week, but it would probably be just his luck to have something happen to keep him there for a couple of weeks or more. And, come to think of it, the doctor had hedged on naming the day. That meant he wasn't tied down to any special time. He could change his mind easily enough and Tom would be stuck.

Robin had said she would come up and study with him, to be sure, but she'd soon get tired of that – especially if he had to stay in the hospital very long. He groaned miserably and squirmed in bed. For the first time self-pity all but overwhelmed him.

Tom was still feeling sorry for himself that evening during visiting hours when Danny and Kay came up to see him.

"Hi, Tom," the young pilot said. "How's it going?"

Tom frowned and returned a halfhearted "All right, I guess,"

"What's the trouble?" Danny asked. "You act as though you just lost your best friend."

"I'm getting tired of staying in this hospital, that's all."

Danny pulled up a chair and sat down beside Kay. "I talked to the doctor a couple of minutes ago, Tom," he said. "He told me that you're getting along fine. I don't believe you're going to be here so very long."

"That's what he keeps telling me," the boy continued, "but I'm beginning to think there's nothing to it. I haven't seen any sign yet that I'm going to get out."

Danny changed the subject and they talked for half an hour or so. Before they left Danny read a portion of Scripture and the three of them prayed together. Danny was the last to pray.

"Dear God," he began quietly, "we know that You often use events to show us Your will and what You would have for us to do. Now, we don't know whether or not You permitted Tom to break his leg in order to show him what You would have him to do, but we pray that if there is a lesson in this thing – if You plan to use this to reveal Your will to him, You will also prepare his heart so he will be ready to follow Your direction."

The words were driven deeply into Tom's heart. Was God using this means to call him to the mission field or to some other form of full-time Christian service? Was that why he fell and broke his leg?

It couldn't be! It wasn't fair! It wasn't fair at all! God knew how badly his dad wanted him to go into the business. He knew that he couldn't go against the wishes of his parents. It wasn't fair to call him into full-time service when he couldn't go!

Tom was so disturbed he scarcely said goodbye when Danny and Kay left, and that night he tossed sleeplessly until one of the night nurses gave him a sleeping pill. Questions raced, unanswered, through his mind.

CHAPTER 9

JACK AND KENT, TROUBLED

Linda Penner had vowed that she would never go out with Jack Ross again, but something seemed to have happened to him over the holidays. Several of the kids talked with her about it.

"Have you been with Jack lately, Linda?" one girl asked.

She shook her head. "Why?"

"I don't know. But I've been watching him lately. He seems sort of different. I don't believe he's driving so fast or talking so loud. And I've noticed in class that he's getting better grades. He's actually doing his homework."

Linda's heart soared. "I haven't heard anything about it," she answered. "Has–has he been going to church somewhere?"

The other girl's eyebrows lifted significantly. "I wouldn't know about that. Don't you think a person can reform without 'getting religion'?"

"Yes, but–" Her voice trailed off into nothingness.

It was two or three days before Linda got a chance to talk to Jack herself. He waited for her just outside the school and walked down the sidewalk with her.

"How are you, Linda?" he asked.

She eyed him questioningly. "I'm fine. How are you?"

His grin seemed more open and friendly than before. "I've never been better," he said.

There was a short silence. "I–I've been hearing some things about you, Jack," she began after a time.

"I suppose Danny has been telling you what a no-good rascal I am."

"Danny hasn't said a word about you," she retorted. "But some of the kids at school have been talking."

He hesitated. "Was it good or bad?"

"They've been wondering what's happened to you, Jack," she went on. "They said you don't drive as fast as you used to and that you're studying better and everything."

He paused and turned to face her.

"How about it?" he asked. "Did you believe them?"

"I don't know why I shouldn't," she said.

"You haven't been very friendly lately."

"That's because–" She swallowed the lump in her throat. "I–I was real happy about it, Jack."

Near the parking lot they stopped once more. He turned to face her. "Are you happy enough about it to start going out with me again?" he asked. There was a strange pleading in his voice.

"I–I don't know. I–"

His frown deepened. "A lot of good it does for me to try to change. You won't believe I can ever be any different than I was, so you won't go out with me."

"That isn't it at all, Jack. It's just that I–"

His lips curled bitterly. "You what?"

Her gaze met his, helplessly. "Please, Jack!"

"A lot of good it does for a guy to try to reform. You just kick him when he's down." He started to turn away. "Now I know it doesn't do any good for me to try to be any different than I've been. You won't go out with me anyway."

"I am glad for what I learned about you, Jack," she said. "Honestly, I am. You've got to believe me."

"Oh, sure! Sure!" Angrily he strode to his car.

Linda remained motionless on the sidewalk until Jack got into his car and drove away. The ache in her heart grew. He was trying to do better. Even the kids at school had noticed it. How could she keep from dating him? And if she did, was she doing the right thing?

Now that Jack was honestly trying to live a clean, respectable life, there might be a chance of leading him to Christ. To be sure, he was trying to clean up his life in his own strength, but he was interested in better things for the first time since she had been acquainted with him. Maybe this was the beginning she had been hoping and praying for. Maybe now she would be able to talk with him about spiritual things and get him to listen. Perhaps she ought to try dating him again.

Slowly Linda walked along the sidewalk toward home. A couple of friends went by on their bicycles and waved to her, but she scarcely saw them.

* * *

At the Orlis home, Kay and Danny noticed a change in Kent too, but it was not for the better. Much of his old arrogance was back. He let up on his studying and left his chores around the house undone. In fact, he acted as though he were doing Danny and Kay a favor by coming home when he was supposed to. He made little effort to hang up his clothes or to clean his feet before going into the house. The first few times he tracked snow across Kay's floor she cleaned up after him and let it go, but finally she got tired of it. Once more he swaggered into the kitchen in snowy boots.

"Hey!" he sang out arrogantly, "got anything to eat around here? I'm about starved!"

Kay came to the doorway. Her gaze swept over the muddy tracks and fastened accusingly on him.

"Kent Gilbert! You didn't take off your boots and I just scrubbed!"

Acting as though he had not even heard her, he walked over to the refrigerator and flung open the door. "Got any decent meat in here?" he demanded. "I can't stand this stuff!"

She grabbed him by the ear gently, but firmly enough so that he knew she meant business.

"Kent Gilbert," she repeated, "you tracked on my newly scrubbed floor."

"I never thought about takin' off my boots," he said, reaching for the meat and butter in the refrigerator. "Get me some bread, will you?"

Kay's voice raised. "Put those things back in the refrigerator and turn around," she ordered. "I'm talking to you."

"But I'm hungry and I haven't had anything to eat yet."

"I don't care if you are hungry. I want you to get those boots off right this minute."

He looked up at her and smirked impudently. "What's the use?" he asked. "The floor's tracked up now."

"I'm not finished." Indignation flashed in her eyes. "Then I want you to get the mop and wash this floor again."

Kent's eyes widened and his lower jaw sagged. "What?"

"You heard me."

Defiance blazed in his young face. "I'm not goin' to do it!" he snorted. "I'm not scrubbin' any floor! And you can't make me!"

At that instant Danny appeared in the kitchen doorway. "Kent, do as Kay says." He spoke quietly, but there was ice in his voice. "Get those boots off and get at that mopping right now."

The boy hesitated uncertainly. Quite deliberately Danny moved toward him. That was all it took. "I–I'm goin'," Kent said quickly. "I'm goin'. You don't need to get so upset about it."

He fled to the back porch where he took off his boots. A moment or two later, his cheeks a fiery red, he came back into the kitchen and began to mop. Danny stood and watched to see that the job was done properly. When Kent finished, Danny called him over.

"Now, Kent," he said sternly, "I don't want you to ever track in like that again."

The boy nodded but did not speak.

"And if I ever hear of you defying Kay and refusing to do as she tells you to do, you'll have to answer to me. Do you understand?"

The boy nodded once more quickly.

"All right. Now you may fix yourself a sandwich if you want to."

* * *

That night after the kids were in bed Danny and Kay sat in the kitchen for a long while talking about Kent and the events of the afternoon.

"I was terribly disappointed, Danny," Kay said. "I thought for a while that he was beginning to make progress. He seemed to be studying better and wasn't nearly as resentful as he had been. But the last few days I've begun to believe I was mistaken about any change in his actions."

Danny pursed his lips. "I'm certainly glad I was home this afternoon when he tried to get away with defying you, Kay."

"So was I."

"That's something you can't let him get away with." Danny continued. "When you tell him to do something, you've got to see that he does it. If you don't, you'll never be able to handle him."

Her mouth was set in a firm line. "I may have been too soft with him at other times, Danny," she said, "but today was one time when he would have done as I told him to. If he hadn't, he'd have wished he had when I got through with him."

Danny laughed. "You know, I believe you mean it."

"You can believe I mean it. It's a hard job cleaning this big kitchen floor. And I'd just finished it when he came tracking in and just stood there, laughing at me."

There was a short silence. "I don't think you'll have to worry about Kent tracking up your floor again. He found out that it was a big job too."

Kay managed a weak laugh. "I was terribly disgusted about the floor, Danny," she said, "but there is something about Kent that disturbs me a great deal more than the trouble we had with him this afternoon."

"Is it something you haven't told me about?" he asked.

She nodded. "I've been suspecting it, but I haven't said anything because I haven't been entirely sure." She paused momentarily. "Danny, I'm almost positive that Kent has started to smoke."

Disbelief flooded the young missionary pilot's eyes. "You can't be serious," he said. "He's such a kid."

"That's what I thought at first. But, Danny, I've been finding tobacco in his pockets, and recently he's started carrying matches."

Danny got to his feet and went to the sink to get a drink of water. "I keep thinking of Kent in terms of my own home life when I was his age," he said slowly. "But we've got to remember that he comes from an entirely different background. I don't suppose his mother and dad cared if he smoked. They probably didn't care what he did."

"I found tobacco in his shirt pocket last week," Kay went on, "or thought I did. But the pieces were so small I couldn't be sure. I checked the shirt he took off yesterday and there's no doubt about it. It's tobacco."

Danny pursed his lips. "Did you say anything to him about it?" he asked.

His young wife shook her head. "I wanted to talk to you first, Danny," she answered. "To tell you the truth, I haven't known exactly what to do."

Danny pulled out his chair and sat down once more pensively. "I'll have a talk with him about it, Kay," he said. "I've always felt that smoking is bad, but since the government released those reports about the harm it does to the body, I think we have an obligation to do what we can to keep kids from smoking – because of that, if for no other reason."

Kay nodded. "And the way I understand it, the younger a person is when he starts to smoke, the greater chance there is of tobacco hurting his body."

Danny took a deep breath. "A boy like Kent, who's so headstrong and wayward, isn't going to pay any attention to the warnings of medical science either," he said. "I'll talk to him about it the first thing in the morning and do what I can. But with a boy like Kent, I can't guarantee a thing."

CHAPTER 10

ROBIN AND JACK HAVE QUESTIONS

Tom had to stay in the hospital until the end of the following week. He thought Robin would soon get tired of coming up to study with him, but she came regularly, bringing him new assignments and taking his completed lessons with hers to school.

"This is great, Robin," he said. "By the time I get back to classes I ought to have most of my work made up."

"That's what we've been working for, isn't it?" she asked, closing her books and leaning back in the chair.

For a couple of minutes he lay there looking at her. "Know something, Robin?" he said at last. "I really think I'm going to get out of here in a few days."

"That will be nice," she replied.

He read the concern in her eyes. "Is there something the matter?"

Her smile came quickly but faded away. "You remember the talks you and I had on the ski trip, don't you?" she asked.

"About full-time Christian service and consecration and things like that?"

She nodded seriously.

"Sure thing. How could I forget them? They've been plaguing me ever since."

"I haven't been able to forget them, either, Tom," she continued. "Every time I pick up my Bible or start to pray, I think about them. I–I've been miserable."

His eyes searched her face. "But I thought you said your parents wouldn't want you to become a missionary."

"They wouldn't." Her voice caught. "That's just the trouble. Mother would cry if I even mentioned it. I don't think she could bear the thought of having me go away from her and Dad – and into the kind of places a missionary sometimes has to go. She would say there's plenty of work to do right here at home."

Tom Channing shrugged. "That ought to settle it then," he said flatly.

"What do you mean?"

"Your parents don't want you to go," he said, "so you shouldn't go. God doesn't expect us to go against the wishes of our parents, does He?"

"I've been trying to tell myself that He doesn't," she said, drawing in a long breath. "But whenever I get to thinking about it, I get such a longing to go that I can hardly stand it. I feel that I've got to follow God's call."

Her words struck him deeply. "You–you aren't real sure that it is God's call, are you?" He paused. "Your parents are Christians, Robin. If becoming a missionary is really God's will for your life, wouldn't God prepare them so they would want you to go?"

"I don't know." Anguish laced her words. "I just don't know."

"I think you're making too big a problem of it, Robin. You're still upset over what happened to us." He hesitated, assembling his words with care. "We're supposed to honor our fathers and mothers. God wouldn't give us a commandment and then tell us to break it, would He?"

She was a long while in answering. "I've tried to make myself believe that I shouldn't go against my parents' wishes, but what if someone wanted to be saved and his parents ordered him not to? Do you think God would expect him to obey them, even though it meant that he would be lost?"

Tom frowned. "What are you trying to say, Robin?" he asked. "Do you mean that we ought to follow a 'call' like yours – if it really is a call – even though our parents don't want us to?"

"The Bible says that we're supposed to love God more than anyone or anything else in the world. If that's true, then He expects us to obey His call, regardless of what anyone else tries to say."

"Even our parents?" Tom asked.

"Even our parents."

The frown on the injured boy's face deepened.

Robin left the hospital early that evening, but Tom didn't care. The evening had been ruined anyway. Even the sleeping pill the nurse gave didn't drive away his anguished sleeplessness.

* * *

In a day or two Jack met Linda as she was going into the snack shop. A smile lit his face.

"Hi, Kitten," he said. "Goin' somewhere?"

"I've been hungry for ice cream all day. I just had to stop by this afternoon and have some."

He followed her inside. "You don't know how lucky you are right now, Linda," he told her. "I'm hungry for ice cream too, and I feel real generous. How about that?"

She sat down in a booth at the back, and he sat across from her.

"I have my own money," she said quietly.

"But you'd like to save it, wouldn't you?"

She smiled at him. Whatever anyone had to say about Jack Ross, she did have to say that he was fun to be with. More fun than any other guy she'd gone out with. And not at all like dating those Christian kids she'd been going out with lately. They were all right, but it was exciting to go with Jack. It was even exciting to sit across from him in the snack shop and listen to him.

Jack did seem genuinely glad to have a chance to talk with her. His voice sounded excited as he told her what he had been doing and asked her about herself and what she'd been doing to have fun the past few weeks. The waitress took their orders and brought their ice cream. When she was gone, they were alone once more. He leaned forward earnestly.

"Tell me something, Linda," he began, "are you going to give me another chance to show you that I'm not the same guy who used to race around town scaring everyone half to death and getting the cops on my tail? Am I going to be able to prove to you that I am different?"

Linda hesitated. "What do you mean?" she asked.

He frowned. "You know what I mean," he retorted. "Are you going to go out with me again? Are you going to let me show you that I'm a good boy now?"

Linda tried swallowing the lump in her throat and pushed nervously at her hair with her hand. "My dad and Elsie don't like you, Jack," she said. "They don't think I should date anyone who isn't a Christian."

He straightened slowly, staring at her. "How can they say you shouldn't go out with me?" he asked. "They don't even know me."

"They've heard about you, Jack, and the wild way you drive."

"But I just told you. I don't drive like that anymore. I'm not the same guy I used to be, Linda. What can I say to make you believe me?"

She hesitated. "You know how I feel about you, Jack," she said. "I used to have a lot of fun going out with you. And–and I'd like to date you again. But

Dad doesn't want me to go with boys who aren't Christians, and I can't go against his wishes."

There was a brief silence. "How does he expect me to become a Christian or whatever you call it," Jack demanded, "if you won't have anything to do with me?"

She felt her cheeks flush. "I–I'd never thought of it quite that way."

"Then you will go out with me?" he pleaded.

"I–I want to pray about it before I give you an answer, Jack," she told him. "I don't know what to do."

He lowered his voice. "Tell you what I'll do," he continued. "If you'll go out with me some Saturday night, I'll go to church with you the next morning. That ought to be fair enough."

Linda's eyes brightened.

"You will?"

"I promise!"

Her face glowed with anticipation. "I–I'll let you know."

Jack sat in the booth for several minutes after Linda was gone. She'd go out with him. He knew she would. Even if he had to go to church with her to get her.

Jack toyed with his spoon. *Come to think of it,* he thought, going *to church won't be such a bad idea at that. It might help to keep anyone from suspecting me.*

His smile broadened. Everything was going just dandy.

Yet, as he got to his feet and started for the cashier, the snack shop door opened, and a uniformed officer stepped inside. Jack cringed and he felt the color drain from his cheeks.

CHAPTER 11

ROBIN'S BURDEN FOR PEGGY

Robin spent busy days making up the homework from the school time she had missed during her stay in the hospital. But, in spite of that, she took time to go to Bible club at Danny and Kay's house. She came in a minute or two late and sat down beside Peggy Merrill, an attractive blond about her own age.

"Hello, Peggy," she said, "I'm glad to see you here tonight."

The other girl smiled in return. "I don't really know why I came." Peggy spoke with disarming frankness. "I certainly didn't plan on it. But it just happened this way."

"It's nice to have you with us, just the same."

"I'd heard some of the kids talking about Bible club," Peggy went on. "But I didn't know much about it and cared a whole lot less until we went on that ski trip. Some of the kids who were at the retreat told me about Bible club and invited me to come and see for myself. I didn't think I'd ever do it, but I didn't have anything else to do tonight, so here I am." She shrugged her shoulders.

"I hope you'll enjoy it," Robin said. "It's one of the highlights of the week for me."

The lesson seemed unusually good that night and Peggy listened intently. She didn't ask any questions, but she leaned forward, clinging to every word.

When it was over and they went into the bedroom to get their coats, she stood quietly by Robin until Robin realized she was waiting.

"Are you walking home alone?" Peggy asked hesitantly.

"I was just going to ask you if you'd like to walk home with me." Robin said.

They put on their coats and went out into the blustery March night together. "If I'd known it was going to be so cold tonight, I'd have tried to get the car," Peggy said.

"We only have a few blocks to walk," Robin told her. "It won't be so bad."

There was a short silence, marred only by the scuffling of the wind through the barren tree branches.

"What did you think of Bible club, Peggy?" Robin asked after a time.

"It was all right, I guess." She breathed deeply. "But Danny said some things I didn't understand very well."

"What were they? Maybe I can help you."

Peggy's lips parted as though she planned to speak, but she checked herself. "It wasn't anything important." She shrugged her shoulders with affected indifference. "I've about forgotten what they were now."

In spite of the fact that she protested her indifference and lack of concern, she was strangely quiet for a time. Finally, Jack drove by slowly, breaking the hush that had fallen between them.

"That's Jack's car, isn't it, Peggy?" Robin asked.

Peggy nodded. "Wonder who he's trying to pick up now?"

"I have an idea he's looking for Linda. You know, she lives in this direction too."

Peggy glanced questioningly at her companion. There was a short silence. "Robin," she said after a time, "would you mind if I ask you something?"

"Not at all."

"Linda is supposed to be a good Christian, isn't she?"

"She is a Christian," Robin answered. "That's true."

"I was sure she was the way she talked during that testimony time, or whatever you call it, on the ski trip. But, if she's a Christian and meant all those things she said that night, why does she go out with a character like Jack?"

"She told me she'd given up dating him," Robin replied. "She said she'd been convicted about going out with him and wasn't going to see him anymore."

"I heard that too," Peggy replied. "In fact, I think

that was one of the things she told two or three of us the night after she gave that speech. But I saw her with him a couple of days or so ago in the snack shop, and the way they were talking and looking at each other, I don't think they've really broken up."

Robin said nothing.

"All of this talk about Christ changing lives sounds great," Peggy went on, "but when I see someone like Linda, I can't help wondering how much of it is talk and how much is the real thing."

Her Christian companion searched for words. "There are times when it's hard for me to understand that sort of thing, too," Robin said. "But our pastor always says that we're supposed to follow Christ, not another Christian."

Peggy shrugged as though it didn't make any difference. "Oh, well, I guess it doesn't matter. It's just something that bothered me a little. That's all."

When they reached Peggy's home a block and a half from Robin's, they stopped for a moment on the walk in front. "I'm glad you came to Bible club tonight, Peggy," Robin said.

"It was sort of interesting."

"Would you like to go to Sunday school and church with me next Sunday?"

Peggy hesitated. "I'd like to, but we have our own church." She started up the walk. "I'll see you, Robin."

Thoughtfully, Robin walked home and into the house. There was something disturbing about Peggy; something she didn't quite understand. It was almost as though she were interested in the things of the Lord but was trying to fight against them.

* * *

Sunday evening Tom came to church on crutches and sat down in the pew beside Robin. She smiled up at him.

"I saw you in church this morning," she said, "and wondered how you've been getting along."

"Great," he told her. "Just great."

The pastor spoke on missions that evening and announced again that the church was having a missionary conference the following week.

"It is our prayer that our church will become more vitally interested in missions through this conference," he said, "and if God is calling any of our young people into this particular vocation, that they will yield to Him."

Tom felt his cheeks flush, and he glanced quickly at Robin. She had looked down, her face flushing crimson.

Tom heard but little of the rest of the message after the announcements. He stared straight ahead, his young face wooden. When it was over and they were going outside he turned once more to Robin.

"A message like that burns me up," he spoke quietly through gritted teeth. "Who does he think he is to tell us what to do? It's not up to him."

The girl at his side responded thoughtfully. "I honestly don't think he meant it that way, Tom."

"Well, that's the way it sounded to me, and I didn't like it!" After a moment he told her that he had his dad's car and asked her if she'd like a ride home.

Robin eyed him curiously. "Won't it bother your leg?"

"No, not at all. I can bend it fine, and I don't have to put any weight on it. Automatic transmissions are great stuff. I'll bet back when they invented them, they didn't think how handy they were going to be for a guy with a leg in such a shape as mine."

Robin laughed. "On the contrary, I'm sure they did. They were undoubtedly thinking just of you when they decided to make cars that way."

They rode around for a short while, talking. Robin told him about Peggy Merrill and shared her concern for her friend. "I don't know why I've been so burdened for her," she said. "But, you know, I haven't been able to think of anything else since Bible club the other night."

Tom thought for a moment or two. "Maybe she's got some problems that are bothering her," he said. "Sometimes there are little things a person will do that show he's upset, even though you don't realize what they are."

"That could be." Robin spoke doubtfully. "But this isn't that sort of feeling. I suppose we can't know positively when the Holy Spirit is dealing with someone, but I can't help thinking that's what is happening with her."

He turned the corner and stopped in front of her home. "Maybe you should talk with her about the

Lord," Tom said, his voice quiet. "You know, Danny says we've got an obligation to witness to others. And especially if God is laying a person on our hearts."

"I'd like to talk to her about Christ," Robin said, "but I–I'm not sure that I know how."

He thought momentarily. "I've read a lot of things that are supposed to help, but when it comes right down to it, I don't know whether any of them would help you now or not. I'll tell you what, though. I'll be praying for Peggy, and for you too, Robin, that God will help you to know what to say to her if you're supposed to talk to her."

"Thanks, Tom." Before he could open the car door, she got out. "It's too hard for you to get around," she said. "I can go to the door by myself."

Her smile was warm and appealing. For an instant or two after she was gone, he sat there without starting the engine. What Robin had told him about Peggy bothered him a great deal.

CHAPTER 12

JACK'S MEETING WITH RILEY

Jack had spent the evening of the Bible club meeting driving around, trying to find Linda. *She must have stayed at home,* he concluded, after half an hour's fruitless search, *or maybe she rode home from Danny and Kay's with somebody else.* He knew this much. If she'd walked, he wouldn't have missed her.

Frowning, he glanced at his watch and noted the time. Riley would be waiting for him. He couldn't keep looking for her now. Reluctantly, he turned at the next corner, drove out to the highway and north to a small cafe on the edge of town. He approached the building slowly, looking up and down the road to be sure that nobody saw him. Then he whipped in, pulled around the ramshackle wooden building and parked in the dark at the rear. Anyone who saw his car here would really have to be out looking for him. And there wasn't much likelihood of that. Kids didn't come to this place much.

For several minutes he sat in the car waiting for Riley to appear. At last a tall, lean-faced individual appeared out of the shadows and sauntered in the direction of the boy's car. Jack rolled down the window.

"Hi, Riley."

The scowling man did not reply.

"I–I didn't know whether you were here or not," Jack continued. "I was just about to give up on you. Thought maybe you couldn't make it tonight."

The gangling man opened the car door and got in. It was a couple of minutes before he spoke. "I was watching you from over there. I just wanted to make sure that you were alone. That's all."

Jack Ross stared at him. "You don't think I'd bring someone else out here when you told me to come alone, do you?" he demanded. "I know better'n that."

"Good." Riley nodded his approval. "But I had to be sure. A guy can't be too careful in this game."

Jack tightened his grip on the steering wheel and breathed deeply. It was a moment or two before he turned again to face his companion. "Well," he said, "what's up? Why did you want to meet me out here tonight?"

"I just wanted to find out how things are going on your end." He lowered his voice. "Everything okay?"

"Everything's fine."

"Is the town quieting down any?"

"Oh sure." Jack spoke with studied carelessness. "You hardly hear anything about the robberies anymore."

"Is that extra cop still on duty?"

"He sure is. But I don't think we have to worry about him. He doesn't know anything."

"Listen," Riley said, "don't ever get the idea that a cop doesn't know anything. You've got to keep your eyes open all the time. See?"

"I have been. But the cops haven't got on to anything. We're all in the clear."

"Good. Good." The icy tone in Riley's voice thawed a little. "What about the kids? Are they still scared?"

"I've had to talk to them to keep 'em in line, but they know nothing's going to happen to us, so they're getting brave again."

"That's the stuff. We're going to need them. You've done a good job, Jack. A real good job."

The boy beamed.

"Do you need some more cash?" the man wanted to know.

Jack laughed nervously. "Do I need more cash? I always need more cash."

"Well, you know how you can get it," Riley said, laughing quietly. "I'm always ready to buy anything you have to sell me and with no questions asked."

Doubt twisted Jack Ross's face. "Do–do you think it's safe?" he asked.

The older man scowled. "If you've been doin' like I told you, of course it's safe."

"I've been doing like you told me, all right. I haven't driven my car at more'n a walk since all the noise got started. And I've been studyin' every night. I've even started gettin' some good grades. And some of the guys even think I've 'got religion.'"

Riley nodded his approval. "That won't hurt a thing. Not a thing. The less attention you call to yourself the better off we'll all be." He took a cigar from his pocket and held it in his hand without lighting it. "Things are quieting down enough now so that you and the boys ought to be able to go to work again before long."

For some reason, uneasiness swept over Jack. For the space of a minute or two he sat behind the wheel of his car, breathing heavily. Sweat pearled on his forehead, and the color fled from his face. Riley noted his reaction and sneered at him, derisively. "What's the matter, Jack?" he taunted. "Are you getting cold feet?"

"Me gettin' cold feet?" The boy swore fervently. "I thought I'd already showed you that I don't get cold feet. I ain't scared of nothin'."

The older man grinned approvingly. "That's the way to talk. As long as you keep your nerve up, you're on top of the world. You've got everything comin' your way. But if you start to chicken out, you'll do something stupid and get us all in a jam."

Jack swore again, as though he were proving that this was his mark of manhood. "Don't you worry about me, Riley. I'm all right. I'm not goin' to let you down."

Riley patted him approvingly on the arm. "I didn't think you would, but a guy in my position can't afford to take any chances. I've got to be sure. You see, I've got my neck in this thing, too. I can't risk havin' this whole thing misfire."

"I'll get the guys together as soon as I can and get things rolling again." Jack spoke softly, and in spite of himself, a slight tremor edged his voice. If Riley noticed it, he said nothing. "You'll be hearing from me one of these days."

The man started to get out of the car, but with his hand on the door, he stopped. "Are you sure you've got your nerve up? You know what it'd mean if you didn't have." Riley drew his forefinger across his throat in an exaggerated cutting motion. "It'd be our necks."

Jack bristled. "How many times do I have to tell you everything's okay with me?"

"What about the girl you were telling me about?" Riley asked. "The one who's supposed to be your alibi. Is that lined up?"

Jack laughed confidently.

* * *

The next day he planned to get in touch with the guys again but as he was on his way to school, Riley drove up beside him as he stopped at a stop sign. He motioned for Jack to roll down his window and, leaning over, tossed him a note. Jack's fingers trembled as he opened and read it.

"Have to go out of town for indefinite period. Hold everything until I get back."

Jack sighed his relief. Until that very moment he had not realized how disturbed he had been at getting the kids together and having them steal again. The hope that Riley would never come back swept over him.

CHAPTER 13

ROBIN'S WITNESS TO PEGGY

During the days after the Bible club meeting, Robin arranged to walk to school with Peggy two or three times. Peggy responded almost hungrily to every offer of friendship.

"It seems strange," she said, "that we've lived so close together all these months, Robin, and only now we're getting to be friends."

"I was thinking the same thing myself yesterday."

They crossed the street and turned toward the high school.

"Tomorrow night's Bible club," Robin said.

"That's right. It is."

"Are you going?"

Peggy looked at her. "I don't know. I really haven't thought much about it."

"Why don't I stop by for you?" Robin suggested.

Peggy paused. "I'll have to think about it. I–I

may have some studying to do." Her answer was halfhearted. She realized that as she spoke, and the embarrassment showed in her face.

Robin eyed her in silence. Guilt and conviction were intermingled on Peggy's young face. Robin's desire to help Peggy came back once more. She ought to speak to her about the Lord Jesus Christ. She ought to talk to her about her need to be saved.

Robin swallowed hard against the tightness in her throat. She had talked with kids before about spiritual things. But up until now it had always been with other Christians – kids who knew what she was talking about and wouldn't ridicule her.

This was different. Peggy Merrill had gone to church. That was true. But all she knew about sin and salvation had been what Danny had said about it at Bible club the week before. Still, she had been most concerned, and after the meeting when Robin walked home with her, she had asked some searching questions that showed she had been thinking most seriously.

The quiet desire in Robin's heart continued. And at last she could ignore it no longer. Praying for courage and the right words, she turned to her new friend.

"Peggy," she said suddenly, "do you mind if I ask you a personal question?"

Her eyes lighted quizzically. "I–I guess not."

Robin grasped her books tightly and continued. "Have–have you ever considered the claims the Lord Jesus Christ has on your life?"

Bewilderment crept into Peggy's eyes. Once or twice she started to talk but stopped before uttering a word. At last she was able to speak. "What do you mean by that?"

"The Lord Jesus Christ came to earth, lived a sinless life, was crucified, and rose again so that you and I can be – saved – if we meet His conditions."

Peggy turned to stare at her. "I suppose all of this means something to you, Robin," she said, "but they're just words to me. I haven't the faintest idea of what you're talking about."

Now that Robin had started, it was fairly easy to continue talking to Peggy about Christ.

"It really isn't as complicated as it sounds. The Bible tells us that we are all sinners – that we all have come short of the glory of God."

The other girl nodded, so Robin continued, "And in another verse it says that *the wages of sin is death.* We're all going to die. Isn't that right?"

"I–I suppose so."

"That's where the story would end if it hadn't been for the Lord Jesus Christ dying on the cross to save us from sin. But God loved us so much that He sent His only Son to bear the guilt of our sin. So, by confessing that we are sinners and putting our trust in Him to save us, we won't have to go to an eternity apart from God when we leave this life. We won't have to go to hell. We can go to heaven and be with Christ."

There was a long, painful silence.

"I–I see." But Peggy's voice was small and weak,

indicating that she actually didn't have a clear idea of what Robin was talking about.

By this time they had reached the school and Peggy seized the opportunity to hurry away. "I've got to run, Robin," she said breathlessly. "I'll see you tonight after school."

"How about Bible club?"

"I'll have to let you know."

* * *

The missionary conference started at church and Tom attended every night. He hadn't planned to go. To be honest, he hadn't even wanted to go, but for some reason, he could not keep from it. He was there every night, sitting well up front, taking notes or marking in his Bible. The messages struck into his life in a way that had never happened before.

At the close of the last service when the invitation was given for those who wanted to consecrate their lives and offer themselves for full-time Christian service, Tom was visibly shaken. Standing there with his head bowed, he grasped the back of the seat ahead of him and squeezed so hard his knuckles whitened and the cords on the backs of his hands stood out.

Although the invitation was actually quite short, it seemed to Tom that it lasted forever. Grimly he fought against it, especially when two or three kids his own age left their seats and went down to the front. *It doesn't matter what anyone else does,* he told himself doggedly. He wasn't going to make a decision to be a missionary. That was all there was to it!

He was not sure how he got through the invitation without going forward. But at last the missionary turned the service back to the pastor, who gave the benediction.

He sighed his relief as he began to file down the aisle toward the door. At last that was over! He shifted his Bible from one hand to the other and pushed his fingers nervously through his hair.

Robin was standing across the church with Peggy. She was as shaken as he was. He could read it in her eyes. For the first time he didn't want to see her, but there was nothing he could do about it. He had to go right in front of them. Their eyes met.

"Hello, Tom."

"Hi!" He forced the corner of his mouth to rise in a halfhearted grin.

"It was a wonderful service tonight, wasn't it?" Robin asked.

He shrugged. "I guess it was all right."

"I thought it was tremendous." A tremor came into her voice. "I've never felt such a pull to go into full-time Christian service as I felt tonight."

"Frankly," he said, "I've never cared for an appeal like that. It was too emotional to suit me."

"Why, Tom!" she exclaimed. "I'm surprised to hear you say that."

"I can't help it. That's the way I feel."

They walked out of the church with him.

"Well," he continued, "I'll be seein' you around." With that he hobbled to his parents' car.

Peggy turned to Robin.

"Tom didn't think much of the service either, so I guess I'm not alone."

"Didn't you like the service?" Robin asked. She tried to keep from showing it, but she felt a sharp disappointment.

"It was all right," the other girl replied lamely, "but I'm like Tom. It seemed to me that the speaker went overboard in trying to get young people to bury themselves in some far-off country with people who don't appreciate them. People who probably don't even want them interfering with their lives."

They started up the sidewalk together.

"The speaker wasn't just bringing his own ideas," Robin said, searching carefully for words. "He was only putting into his own words what the Bible has to say about missionary work. The Bible tells us that it is our responsibility to spread the gospel to everyone – to every place in all the world." She breathed deeply. "We really can't argue with it. It's a command from God."

"But why?" Peggy asked with all seriousness.

"Because every person who doesn't confess his sin and put his trust in the Lord Jesus Christ is lost," the young Christian said.

Peggy's brow furrowed. "Do you mean to tell me that some poor African who has never heard the story of–of–Jesus–" Her voice faltered over the name, and it was a second or two before she could continue. "Do you mean to say that a person like that is–is lost?"

"That's right."

"I've never heard anything like that before."

"Of course you have," Robin continued. "The missionary explained it this evening. He said that God has placed in the hearts of all peoples everywhere some idea about what is right and what is wrong. But they don't even live up to the little light they have. They can't even keep the few laws they do understand."

"It just doesn't seem right."

"We had a missionary in our home who told us that every tribe he had come in contact with in Africa had some sort of a code to live by. He said that he had never met a man who honestly could say that he didn't know he was a sinner. So," Robin concluded, "if they are sinners, they have earned the wages of sin, which is death, just like the people here in America."

Peggy was a long while in answering.

"Like me?" she said numbly, her voice scarcely sounding the words.

Robin nodded. "Like you," she said softly.

Peggy thought about that for a moment. "I don't think I've been so bad," she countered after a time. "I may not have been a hundred percent perfect, but I've certainly tried to do what's right. I don't think I've done enough bad things to be worthy of–of–" She could not even force herself to say the word.

"It doesn't matter at all what you or I think, Peggy," Robin went on gently. "The only thing that really matters is this. 'What does the Word of God say?' There's no arguing with the Bible. And there's no mistaking it either. It is very clear on these points. Everyone in the world is a sinner and is going to hell unless he confesses his sin and puts his trust in the Lord Jesus Christ to save him."

The other girl took a deep breath. "I just don't understand it."

"I understand how you feel, Peggy. Would you like to go with me to talk to the pastor? I'm sure he could answer your questions."

"Oh, no!" Fright leaped within her. "I wouldn't think of that." She glanced quickly at her watch. "I've got to run. I should have been home twenty minutes ago."

Desperately, but without success, Robin searched for something to say.

CHAPTER 14

TOM FACES CONFLICT

Tom hobbled over to the car on his crutches and got into the back seat to wait for his parents. The message was still burning fiercely in his heart.

Mrs. Channing was the first to speak when they started home. "Wasn't that a challenging message?" she asked of no one in particular. "It almost made me wish I was young again so I could go out as a missionary."

She sighed deeply.

Tom squirmed. His father did not speak until he turned onto the street where they lived.

"Yes," he said, "it was a good presentation of the work of missions," he said. "In fact I can't remember when I've ever heard better. It made me realize that we've all got a responsibility to those who have never heard the gospel. I'm not saying this for publication or because I'm especially proud of it, but I was so touched I put a check for several hundred dollars in the offering."

"I'm so proud of you, dear," his wife said. "I was just thinking – I believe I'll wait a while before getting new drapes and send that money over to the pastor – that is, if you don't mind."

"Mind?" he echoed. "I'm proud of you."

All this time Tom had said nothing. Finally Mrs. Channing looked back at him. "What did you think of the message, Tom?"

His mouth worked uneasily, and he turned and began to fiddle with the door-locking device on his side.

"Tom," his dad said, "what did you think of the service tonight?"

"It was all right, I guess." His voice faltered.

Immediately his mother whirled to face him. "Is there something wrong?"

"Wrong?" Tom acted as though there couldn't possibly be any kind of difficulty. "What makes you think there's something wrong?"

"I don't know," she answered. "You're so quiet this evening that you worry me. I can't help wondering if you're sick or something."

Mr. Channing stopped in the driveway, and they all got out and went into the house, where they sat down in the living room.

"You don't look as though you feel very well, Tom," his mother repeated.

"I'm not sick," he retorted. Then his voice softened. "I–I'm sort of like you and Dad. That message tonight sure got a hold of me."

Mr. Channing smiled. "I guess we're all agreed that I did the right thing when I put that check in the offering," he said. "You can feel that you're having a part in missions too, Tom. The gift is from all of us." He paused significantly. "In fact, since mother is giving up her drapes, I'll send along another gift to be from you, personally."

Tom Channing swallowed hard. "That's not exactly what I was thinking about, Dad," he said, stammering.

"What do you mean?"

"The missionaries have been talking all week about how badly men are needed on the mission fields everywhere." He raised his gaze to meet theirs. "I've been thinking that perhaps I–I–"

Disapproval was evident in their eyes. His mother was the first to speak. "Surely you–you're not serious," she said, her voice trembling.

"I–I've been sort of thinking about the mission field these past few weeks."

Mr. Channing snorted indignantly. "I've never heard of anything so ridiculous," he exclaimed. "Do you know what kind of a place you'd be living in, Tom? Do you know how much money you'd make? As soon as you graduate from high school and college, you've got your work cut out for you helping me to run our business. There's plenty of work to do right here in Fairview without getting some wild idea about running off to some other country."

Tom's jaw was set firmly. "But, Dad," he countered,

"if God has been speaking to me about it, I–I don't see how I can stay here."

His father got imperiously to his feet. "Now, Tom. Let's have no more of this nonsense from you. You're just stirred emotionally by the things that were said tonight. Don't let yourself get all upset. You'll feel altogether different about it in the morning."

With that he strode into another part of the house to end the conversation.

Tom stared miserably after him.

CHAPTER 15

PEGGY DECIDES

Robin went to bed that night at her usual time but could not sleep. Every time she closed her eyes, she could see Peggy's earnest young face. If only she could have said the right words, she was sure that Peggy would have made a decision for Christ. She was so close – so very close.

At last Robin slipped out of bed and knelt in prayer for her new friend. She was still praying when the phone rang. The sudden noise startled her. She got to her feet and started toward the phone, but her father got there first.

"It's for you, Robin," he said irritably. "I can't imagine why anyone would be calling at this hour." She went to the phone.

"Robin, this is Peggy!" The girl's voice was so distraught that Robin could scarcely understand what she was saying. "Can you come right over?"

"Come over?" Robin asked. "Why, it's almost midnight."

"I know, but I can't sleep or anything." Peggy stifled a sob. "Robin, will you come over and show me how to accept Christ as my Savior? I want to be a Christian!"

Robin quickly whispered to her father what the situation was. He touched her on the shoulder and whispered back, "Tell her you'll be there as soon as you can."

When she finished talking with Peggy, Robin went in and got dressed quickly. Mr. Evans put on his pants, shoes, and a robe. "I'll drive you over to Peggy's house."

"But it's not even two blocks away. I can walk."

"Not on an errand like this." He patted her shoulder affectionately. "If I can't take you to talk to a friend about her relationship to Christ, I'm not much of a Christian father."

She climbed into the car and sat silently until he stopped the car at the Merrill home.

"Call when you're finished, dear."

She nodded. "Be praying for me, Daddy," she said in desperation. "I don't have the slightest idea of what to say!"

She walked quickly to where Peggy was waiting for her. Quietly and in the dark, Peggy let her in by a side door. "I hated to get you up like this, but I–I just have to talk to someone tonight."

"That's all right," Robin answered.

"We've got to be extra quiet," Peggy said guardedly. "I don't want to wake my parents."

Stealthily they tiptoed up to her room and she closed the door.

"It was lucky for me that I have a phone in my room and that Mom and Dad sleep on the other side of the house on the first floor."

They sat down in the dim half-light of her bedroom. She had not turned on the light, but the street light on the corner dispelled most of the darkness.

"What do you want to talk to me about, Peggy?" Robin asked.

"Everything!" Peggy exclaimed. "Robin, I don't want to go to hell. I don't want to be lost!"

"You don't have to be." Robin's voice sounded the confidence that she suddenly felt. "Nobody has to be. God provided a way to escape. All you have to do is to confess your sin and put your trust in the Lord Jesus Christ to save you."

"That's what I want to do, more than anything else in the world."

But Robin did not pray with her immediately. She went over the way of salvation slowly, quoting Bible verses and asking questions until she was sure that Peggy understood. Then they knelt together, and Peggy gave her heart to the Lord Jesus Christ. After that they both cried a little and, for a time, whispered in the darkness.

"You'll never know how thankful I am that you came over this evening, Robin," she whispered. "I hated to call you. But I–I just couldn't stand it any longer. I felt that I couldn't let another night go by without confessing my sin and becoming a Christian."

Robin smiled her own happiness. "You couldn't have done anything that would have made me any happier. And I mean that. I don't know whether I'll be able to sleep the rest of the night or not."

"Neither do I."

Excitedly Robin told her dad what had happened as she sat in the car beside him on the way home. "Oh, Dad, it was wonderful!" she exclaimed. "Peggy accepted Christ as her Savior."

"Praise the Lord!"

"I'm so happy I–I don't think I can stand it!"

"That's a thrill that doesn't come to enough Christians, Robin," he went on. "If we all would witness the way you did to Peggy, I'm sure we'd have the same thrill you've had tonight. We probably would have it many times if we were only faithful to God in our opportunities to witness."

For a brief space of time Robin sat there in silence. "It–it almost makes me want to spend my whole life talking to people about the Lord," she murmured.

A strange, defensive tone came to her father's voice. "What do you mean?"

"It almost makes me feel as though I ought to answer the call of God," she said, "to–to become a missionary."

His hands tightened on the wheel and, although he stopped at the house, it was a minute or so before they got out and went inside.

"You can do a lot of witnessing right here in Fairview, Robin."

She looked at him, the hurt growing inside her.

"I don't think I know what you mean, Daddy." And yet she did know what he meant. Down in her heart she knew. But she did not want to admit it.

"The town's full of people like Peggy," he said. "They're lost and need the Savior. You could talk to them the way you talked to Peggy tonight. Just think what a lot you could do for Christ right here at home."

"But that's not the same." She tried desperately to find the words to say what she felt within, but it didn't come out very forcefully. "God is calling me into full-time Christian service."

Mr. Evans' face showed his tenseness, but he managed a smile.

"You're just touched by the emotional appeal that was made at church tonight," he said, "and by the joy of helping Peggy to find Christ as her Savior. You'll feel entirely different about all of this in the morning."

"It isn't that."

He bent over and kissed her affectionately on the tip of the nose.

"Well, we're not going to let an argument spoil our happiness tonight. We can go into this some other time."

Reluctantly she started for her bedroom. The elation she had felt at being able to help Peggy was gone. A new dejection had replaced it.

"Good night, Daddy," she said as though a great weariness had overtaken her.

"Good night, dear." When she reached the doorway to her room, he spoke again. "And, Robin, please don't say anything to your mother about what you and I were just talking about – at least for a while. It would break her heart to think that you were even considering going away from Fairview – and especially to become a missionary."

Robin went back to bed, but it would have been just as well had she stayed up. Sleep refused to come.

Why can't my parents understand the call in my heart? Why can't they realize that God has called and I have to go? Robin's questions came back to her, unanswered, in the dark.

The next morning she was up an hour before her usual time. She dressed, took her Bible, and curled up in a chair in the living room and began to read. Her mother found her there, asleep, when she got up at 6:30. She sat down on the arm of the chair and kissed her awake.

"Now, what's this all about, Robin?" she asked, speaking gently. "Why are you sleeping out here?"

The girl straightened, scrubbing the sleep from her eyes. For an instant or two she looked around numbly.

"I–I must have fallen asleep."

"Daddy told me what happened last night," she said. "I was lying awake all the time, praying for you and Peggy." She kissed her again. "We're both so very proud of you for what you've done, Robin."

"It wasn't anything I did."

"You testified," her mother continued, "and God was able to use your testimony. It makes me feel that our Christian lives have been worthwhile when we know that we have a daughter who is close enough to Christ to be used." Her smile was genuine.

"I don't feel as though I've done anything so wonderful," Robin said, her voice revealing her uneasiness.

"That's just like you, not wanting to take credit for yourself. You're not only zealous for the Lord and wanting to lead people to Him, but you're modest as well."

A sudden revulsion all but overwhelmed Robin. "Oh, Mom!" she exclaimed. "Please!"

After breakfast Robin called Peggy and made arrangements to stop by and walk to school with her.

"I was just going to call you," the new Christian said. "Could you come a little early? There are some things I'd like to talk to you about."

Robin glanced up at the kitchen clock. "I can be there in about five minutes," she replied, "if you can be ready then."

Peggy was waiting for her on the front steps when Robin arrived. They walked toward the school together.

"How do you feel this morning?" Robin asked her.

Her new friend turned slightly. "That's what I wanted to talk to you about. Everything was so wonderful last night after I made my decision to become a Christian that I thought I couldn't possibly be any happier. But to be honest with you, Robin, I don't feel any different this morning than I did yesterday."

"That's understandable."

Disappointment clouded Peggy's face. "But I thought I'd *feel* different," she went on.

"In what way?"

"I don't know for sure. I thought I'd be happier, for one thing, and want to think and talk about spiritual things all the time. But I don't. What happened last night seems so unreal – almost like a dream."

"But it wasn't a dream," Robin countered. "You made a decision last night. You confessed your sin and accepted Christ as your personal Savior."

There was a brief silence, then Peggy stopped and faced Robin. "You talk about how wonderful it is to be a Christian and how close a person feels to God, but to be completely honest with you, Robin, I haven't noticed any difference at all," Peggy went on. "This morning I woke up early and tried to read the Bible and pray. I thought I'd enjoy it so much, but I didn't. I couldn't even understand it. Frankly, I feel sort of let down and disappointed today."

Robin thought for a moment before speaking. "Danny has talked about that in Bible club from time to time," she said, "and so has Pastor Bracken. They say that a lot of people feel that way after they've made a decision for the Lord Jesus Christ." She took a deep breath. "The thing is, we're saved by confessing our sin and putting our trust in Christ – not by our feelings. So, how you feel today doesn't change things a bit. You're a Christian now."

Peggy's forehead crinkled questioningly. "But if I am different, I ought to feel different, hadn't I?"

Robin weighed carefully what her friend had said. "Didn't you tell me that you and your parents came here from Canada and are going to become American citizens?"

"Yes," Peggy answered, "but I don't see what that's got to do with it."

"Tell me, did you feel any different when you moved here?"

She shook her head.

"Do you think you'll feel any different when you get your American citizenship papers?"

"I don't know. I don't suppose we will."

"But things will be different, whether you feel they are or not," Robin went on. "If you ever travel to a foreign country, you'll have to go on an American passport. It's the same way spiritually. You've trusted Christ as your Savior, so you're a Christian. It's as simple as that."

Peggy nodded. "I think I'm beginning to see what you mean."

"There are plenty of Bible verses that will prove what I've said," Robin continued, "but I don't know them well enough to quote them to you. I do know, though, that it's true."

Peggy took her friend's hand and squeezed it impulsively. "You've helped me more than you'll ever know."

CHAPTER 16

ROBIN EVANS, COMMITTED

The same morning, Jack Ross received a message from Riley, who wasn't going to be able to come back for a while. He stuffed his phone into his pocket and waited for Linda. The words of Riley's message flashed in his mind. "But I want you to get to dating that 'chick' again. The one who's going to furnish you with an alibi. There's no telling when you're going to need it."

That was one piece of advice that would be easy to follow. The fact is he'd missed her during the time they hadn't been going out together. Maybe after he and Riley had finished their business, he could really start going out with Linda again. That religion bit of hers would give him a bad time, but he ought to be able to get around it somehow. He'd always been able to get around everything else when it came to her.

He was still standing there thinking about her when she came walking by. "Hi, Kitten," he said, grinning.

Her eyes laughed at him. "Just what are you doing out here?"

"I decided I'd just park the old chariot along your way to school and wait till you came by. Long time, no see."

She dimpled, smiling happily. "You just haven't looked very hard, that's all."

"How about a date tomorrow night?"

She hesitated. "I don't know, Jack," she said uncertainly. "I've got a lot of studying to do."

"You promised."

"I didn't promise to go out with you," she reminded him. "I promised to think about it."

"Well, you've had time to think about it," he went on. "What're you goin' to do now? Are you goin' out with me or not?"

She did not answer him.

"Well, how about it? What're you goin' to do?"

"I don't know what to say."

He stepped closer and lowered his voice. "I'll go to church with you this Sunday morning if you'll go with me tomorrow night. Now, how's that for a deal?"

"I–I'd like to have you go to church," she said, "but going just so I'll go out with you isn't the right reason."

He stared at her angrily. "I don't know what more you could want!" He whirled and stormed back to his car.

Linda walked on toward the school alone. The color flooded her cheeks, and her hands were trembling. She couldn't understand why Jack Ross affected her that way.

In the car Jack started the engine and roared up the street, unmindful of Riley's instructions about driving decently. That Linda! Since she became a Christian, she was no fun at all! Now he and Riley couldn't pull off the jobs they'd planned. They'd have to cancel them!

* * *

The next week when Bible club met at the Orlis house Peggy went with Robin. Danny and Kay had already heard that Peggy had made a decision for Christ but did not ask her about it in front of the others. But when the meeting was over Robin and her new friend lingered behind the others. As soon as possible Kay went over to her.

"We heard some wonderful news about you, Peggy," she said.

The blond girl smiled with a friendliness she had never shown before. "That's what we wanted to talk with you about."

Danny, who had been standing at the door with some of the guys, said goodbye and turned to join Kay and the girls. He looked from one to the other quizzically.

"You look as though you have something on your minds."

"We do have," Robin said. "That's why we stayed to talk to you. We felt that you would be able to help us.

"We'll certainly do what we can."

"I tried to explain to Peggy about this matter of 'feeling' saved," she went on, "but I wasn't able to quote any Bible verses to back up what I told her. We thought probably you could help us if we asked you about it."

"I see," Danny answered.

"I accepted Christ as my Savior last night," Peggy said, "but today I've had such a letdown feeling. To be truthful, it's made me wonder whether I wasn't just overemotional. After it happened, I was so happy and I thought I was going to be that way all the time, but I don't feel any different than I did before." She breathed deeply. "Of course, the things she told me helped some, but we thought if you could show us what the Bible has to say about it–"

Danny smiled. "I think some of us Christians make a big mistake," he began, "when we tell the unsaved how wonderful everything will be once they accept Christ as their Savior. Of course, it's true that it is wonderful to be a Christian. A person can't be truly happy unless he does know Christ as his Savior.

"But it's so easy for someone who is a new Christian to get the mistaken impression that the Christian life is all 'feeling,' and if they don't have a wonderful feeling all the time they aren't saved.

"The first thing we've got to understand is that we are saved. Paul wrote: *For I know whom I have believed, and am persuaded that he is able to keep that which I have committed unto him against that day."*

Danny and Kay quoted other Bible verses to explain and lend support to what they were saying. Peggy nodded from time to time.

"I'm beginning to understand now," she said.

At last the girls got to their feet and started to leave, but Kay asked them to wait a moment.

"You know," she said, "there is one thing you girls could do together that would help you both, but especially Peggy."

"What's that?"

"I'd like to suggest that both of you take an online Bible course."

Peggy looked questioningly at her Christian friend. "I–I'd like to," she said, "but I don't think it would do me any good. I don't know anything about the Bible."

"We could study together," Robin suggested.

"That would be fun."

"I'll look for a course the first thing in the morning," Robin went on. "And as soon as we can, we'll get together and study the first lesson. Maybe we can do one a week."

They talked on for half an hour or so, and when they finally left, Danny turned to Kay.

"There's a girl who's going to become a mature Christian. She's hungry for the Word of God and insists on getting answers to her questions."

"I was thinking the same thing," Kay replied. "Peggy's going to be a real witness here in Fairview."

* * *

The following evening Robin and her parents were still sitting at the dinner table where they had been for almost an hour.

"Did Robin tell you that she's going to help Peggy with a beginner's Bible course?" Mr. Evans asked his wife.

Mrs. Evans nodded. "I was talking with Peggy's mother this afternoon," she replied. "Mrs. Merrill is quite disturbed about what's happened to Peggy. She doesn't understand it at all."

"Peggy said she'd been talking to her parents about it all," Robin put in.

"Her mother was very gracious when I tried to explain just what it means to be saved, but she can't grasp it. All she could say was that her church had never taught her anything like that."

"It's like I was telling Robin," Mr. Evans said. "There are so many people right here in Fairview who don't know Christ as their Savior that the Bible-preaching churches haven't even begun to scratch the surface. I believe a young person could work her whole lifetime right here in our own little town and do a lot for the Lord without going off to some foreign country."

Robin flinched at his remarks and glanced quickly at her mother. Mrs. Evans sat up straight and slowly returned her coffee cup to the table.

"Just what do you mean by that?" she demanded pointedly.

"Not much of anything," he said. For a moment his cheeks colored. "We–we were just talking about missions and people going out as missionaries, and I thought of what a tremendous mission field we have right here in Fairview."

But Mrs. Evans was not to be put off. She sensed that there was more as she looked from her husband to Robin. "Robin," she said, "You–you aren't thinking of going off somewhere as a missionary, are you?"

The girl eyed her pleadingly and stumbled in her search for words.

"Are you?"

"I–I don't know, Mom," she answered miserably. "I want to serve God in some way and I–I've been wondering if He might be calling me into some kind of Christian service."

Her mother stared rigidly ahead. "You're all we have," she said. Desperation stole the life from her voice, and she spoke hesitantly. "If you should go away, I–I don't think I'd be able to stand it!"

Mr. Evans eyed his wife helplessly. "Don't get so upset, dear. All Robin said was that she wants to serve God in some way. It's like I was saying, there's no need for her to go anywhere. There's plenty of Christian service that needs to be done right here in Fairview."

"I know you're right," she answered, "but I just can't stand to think about Robin going away and leaving us. Why, if she went to the mission field, we might never see her again! Have you ever thought of that?"

"Don't worry about it. Robin hasn't gone yet." He pushed back from the table. "We're going to have to hurry or we'll miss prayer meeting."

Mrs. Evans leaned down and impulsively kissed Robin on the cheek.

Robin was still sitting at the table when they left the house. The ache in her heart continued to grow. *Perhaps what Dad said about Fairview is true,* she thought. *In fact, sure it is. But that doesn't mean that God is calling me to do anything about Fairview – as a lifework, that is. He is calling me to full-time Christian service as a missionary.*

She got to her feet and walked thoughtfully into the other room. She knew what God wanted her to do. She knew what she wanted to do. But how could she follow His leading when her parents were so opposed to it?

* * *

Mr. and Mrs. Evans drove slowly up the street and through the business district to the church.

"Do you think Robin is actually serious?" Mrs. Evans asked, turning toward her husband.

His grip tightened on the steering wheel and his eyes narrowed.

"About what?"

"About becoming a–a missionary." The words caught in her throat.

"She's just thrilled over leading Peggy to the Lord," he continued, "and thinks it would be so much fun to do the same thing every day. Don't worry, dear. After a little while she'll get over it."

Mrs. Evans twisted the handles on her purse. "It–it's not that I object to giving her to the Lord or anything like that," she continued. "And I know you're as thrilled as I was when we found out that she loves Christ enough to want to lead others to Him. But I–I just don't think I can stand it if she should decide to be a missionary and go to some terrible place like Africa or Borneo, and I'd have to face up to the fact that we–we might never see her again. Do you realize what that would be like?"

The corners of his mouth tightened. "That's just what I've been thinking, and I've got to admit it's not very pleasant. But how many different things did you plan to be when you were young? Answer me that."

In spite of herself she smiled weakly.

"Robin thinks she wants to be a missionary now," Mr. Evans continued. "Tomorrow it will probably be a nurse or a doctor or a flight attendant. And she'll undoubtedly end up marrying a boy up the street and settling down right here in Fairview."

"I wish I could be sure of that." Mrs. Evans spoke uncertainly. "But Robin has never been one to do a lot of talking about what she's going to do, and she's not easily changed once she makes up her mind to something."

They parked near the church and got out.

"I'd feel altogether differently about it if she were stronger," her mother went on. "But she's so frail and delicate. Robin would never be able to stand a harsh climate. She'd break under it."

"I've always thought she was more healthy than most kids her age," her dad said. "She's never sick."

"That's because I've protected her. You don't know how closely I've watched her to see that she doesn't catch cold or eat the wrong food or–or do something else that wouldn't be good for her." She sighed deeply. "If Robin were to go somewhere as a missionary, I just don't think she'd be able to live through her first term without breaking completely."

When it came time for prayer that evening, Mrs. Evans had an unspoken prayer request.

And in another part of the town, Robin, who was at home, knelt and poured her heart out to God.

"Dear God," she prayed, "please work in the lives of Mom and Dad, and help them to decide it's best for me to follow Your direction and go out as a missionary."

For her the battle was over – at least for the moment. She was going to follow God's will for her life.

When she got to her feet the warmth of complete happiness swept over her.

www.ingramcontent.com/pod-product-compliance
Lightning Source LLC
Chambersburg PA
CBHW060502300726
48975CB00008B/2616